# Shadow in the Witch House

The Chronicles of Randy Carter Book 2

Sonya Lawson

SauceBox Press

# CONTENTS

This book contains scenes that may depict, mention, or discuss abusive relationships, animal abuse, animal death, assault, attempted murder, blood, bullying, cheating, child abuse, cults, death, divorce, emotional abuse, fatphobia, gun violence, homophobia, hospitalization, misogyny, murder, sexism, and/or violence. Please take care of yourself as you read.

To Lynn, a Columbus native. We may not be blood, but you'll always be my sister.

# ONE

RESTING MACARONS FOR AT least forty-five minutes before putting them in the oven was crucial. It was during this period they formed their skin, then the hardened outer layer got more solid in the flames of the oven and created the slightly tough bit. Gave the macaron a delicious crackle and snap on the first bite. It was the rough edge right before the ooey-gooey middle of the cookie and the sweet richness of the inner cream—ganache, buttercream, jam... whatever was stuffed in the middle there.

The skin was key, which meant so was the hardening part. The process made it tough enough to come out of the oven just right. If macarons weren't a perfect metaphor for the shitstorm of my life, and the hope I had that I'd come out tougher but still good, I didn't know what would be.

BACK TO WHERE I was: still maybe a wee bit in shock from the events that had taken down the black church and what we'd hoped was the seed of Starry Wisdom's power. It was still before the complex set of emotions I had about leaving Macy for dead in the shadow world—namely relief mixed with guilt mixed with a bunch of bitch-had-it-coming—had a chance to fully set... but after Nyarlathotep—the Prince of the Dreamlands turned from starry lion to slightly goth hot dude—showed at my café, all golden-brown, smooth skin and piercing night-sky eyes and power, making my own magical thrum purr in my chest.

Harley and Gareth were still appropriately freaked out by him. Any sane person who knew something of Outer Gods or magic should've been. I'd never claimed to be fully sane, so I'd invited him out for a drink. Partially because my magic somehow compelled me toward him. Something in me reached out for him when I was in his presence. Partially because he hinted all the blood and magic we shed back in Upper Arlington wasn't enough to take out the baddies who were behind the Starry Wisdom cult.

Harley pushed Merry and Mia into her slick, black luxury sedan against their very vocal protests. My sisters didn't know who Nyarlathotep was, but they would fight tooth and nail to stay by my side if they caught even the faintest whiff of trouble. Harley, fully invested in my sisters now that she was dating Merry and obviously happy about it, took no prisoners. Standing in my café, facing off with the stubborn might of two-thirds of the Carter sister clan, Harley held her ground. She crossed her arms over her chest, looked them over, and visibly deflated. Rubbed her hand over her brow and said, "I'm tired. I'm sure Randy and Gareth are as well. They need to have a discussion, but none of us can do what we need to do and get the rest we need if you don't agree to get yourselves safe."

Merry and Mia shuffled their feet, handed out fierce hugs and a few side-eye glares, and let plenty of mumbles and grumbles rip, but they exited after Harley's little speech. Lucky for her, they didn't see her look back at me with a wink, or the pep in her step as she followed them out of the back kitchen door. I held in a laugh, but barely. She was already fitting into the Carter family so well; guilt trips were a standard weapon in our family arsenal.

Harley's words had implied it, but Gareth's hard eyes and rigid stance confirmed he was going nowhere. If I was going to chat it up with the Outer God Nyarlathotep, he was coming along for the ride. I didn't bother questioning either man. Harley had been right about one thing. I was tired and wanted to get to my bed in the near future.

"Come on then," I said to no one in particular as I walked to the back of my café. I called back, "Lock the door back, would ya?" as I grabbed my wristlet and keys from their place by the back door and exited into the warm night, waiting for the men to follow so I could lock up behind us. We had plenty of wards around the place, but I was fuzzy on whether they protected from magical enemies and dangers or all types of dangers, like a run-of-the-mill burglar. Another thing I needed to add to my ever-growing list titled "Shit Randy Should Probably Know about Magic if She Wasn't Clueless."

As I led the way to a bar a block down, Gareth stepped to my left to be my shield from the street. Nyarlathotep stepped up to my right, his appearance easy and sexy but his eyes cunning and alert. Add their power to the fact both of them made my skin buzz with lust and other things—Gareth with his quiet, calming influence despite his outward buff, blond biker vibe and the Prince with his thrum of power that sent my own into hyperdrive—and I was feeling a little light-headed from all the sensations as we made our way through the doors of the bar.

It was late-ish, and Thursday nights in the Old North stayed crowded. OSU being a handful of blocks up on High Street and Thursday forever ingrained as the start of every American college student's weekend made North High a bustling place close to midnight on any given Thursday. The sports bar we entered was no exception. There was no room at the bar and no tables open in the small space around the bar and pool tables.

I sagged a little at the sight, ready to sit with a beer and at least take a physical load off for a damn moment. Gareth moved to speak, but Nyarlathotep beat him to the punch. "Allow me," he said with a wicked grin, and he slipped through the throng toward the full tables at the back.

"Do you think..."

I brushed off Gareth's worried tone. "I hardly think he's going to cause chaos and carnage in a sports bar tonight, Gareth. Outside total destruction, I'm fine with him getting us a table."

Gareth gritted his teeth but nodded, his eyes softening as he stepped closer. His body hugged mine as he dipped his mouth down to whisper, "Are you sure you're up to this? You can tell him to fuck off, at least for now."

"A charming thought, boy, but our Randy is made of sterner stuff, no?" The Prince said, popping up out of nowhere, somehow juggling three full pint glasses in his hand. "Follow me," he said before either of us could answer, making a path for us through the crowded room, right up to an empty table in a dark corner. Guess it was good to have compelling magical powers in a crowded bar.

"She's been through a lot today," Gareth rumbled in his deep voice, scooting his chair so it sat firmly between me and the Outer God.

"*She* is sitting right here, big guy, and *she* can speak for herself," I said before taking a long pull from the cold beer and letting the chill drip down my throat, fill the pit of my stomach, and shimmer through me. "But, yes, I'm tired and not in the mood to play games, so whatever your god-ness wants with us, please spit it out so I can find my bed."

Nyarlathotep's smile widened when I said the word "bed," but he made no innuendos. Instead, he twirled a hand loosely in the air and the sound of the buzzing bar muted. It was like the spell Macy had pulled in my café, which made my body shiver in a not-so-fun way.

"As I was trying to explain in your café, we currently have a common enemy."

"Starry Wisdom?" I asked.

"Yes, and no. Starry Wisdom is the human arm of our enemy, but the humans don't pull the strings. They don't make the grand, awful plans. Something with far more power behind it does. Likely another Outer God."

"That narrows the field," Gareth said.

"Too true. There are but four of us. I know I didn't kidnap myself, which leaves my sire and my two siblings. None are good options."

"Why?" I asked, still a little too out of the loop when it came to the Outer Gods mess.

The charming Prince—though I knew he was no Prince Charming—sat back and winked. "They aren't nearly as fun as me," he said before taking his own deep pull of beer. His eyes turned darker, a move I would've called impossible if I hadn't seen it for myself, and he said in a firm tone, "I am the only Outer God who can travel to the human plane. The only one who should, because the others are creatures of pure ego and destruction."

"Why should we believe you, Crawling Chaos?" Gareth countered.

"The old names never get old, and they hint at what I can be, but believe me when I say, boy, I am far more apt to help humans than to harm them. The others, however, would have no qualm burning all of humanity alive to sit atop the ash heap left in their wake."

"What makes you so different?" I asked. He didn't owe me an explanation or anything. To be honest, my question was more about myself than anything, because I knew we had all this weird magical ability in common.

"My continual contact with humans within and outside of time, possibly. I do not fully know myself."

"I'm hesitant to believe any of this," Gareth said.

"As you rightly should be," Nyarlathotep replied. "However, in this case, it might be good to ease out of such skepticism quickly."

"Okay, even if I were to say I believe you; you're not all about Starry Wisdom, but some other god is pulling the strings. Why exactly can't you take care of it? I mean..." I trailed off, waving a hand vaguely at him. "An awful lot of power you're packing."

"I pack more than power, sweetling," he purred in response, which made Gareth shift in his seat.

I stared at him, ignoring his comment so he'd get to the point.

"Very well, lovely. All this power you feel? It's a fraction of my usual power. My human form and my beast form have joined again, thanks to you freeing me tonight, but I am still missing parts of my power. Always do in my human form, but more is missing in me. Namely, the parts secreted away in the Book of Knowing."

"Which is?" I asked.

"The book gives him omniscience," Gareth answered.

"Mostly correct, but not exactly. It allows me to see and know things, past, present, and future, if I ask the proper questions. It also holds slivers of my power, ones I imbued into its pages to allow me to use it properly. Whoever split me took additional magics from me, sucked them away as they snatched the book from its place in the inbetween. I'm still powerful, yes. Still a force. Yet not nearly enough to confront a member of my family."

"Once again, we come back to the question: What's all this have to do with us?" I asked.

"Whoever took from me is controlling Starry Wisdom. Erasing the black church was a blow to their power, but they are not gone."

"I left their leader to be eaten by monsters in the shadow world, so..."

He interrupted me with a look I might call beseeching if I thought a being like him would need to beseech me for any reason. "She was their human leader, but there are many who serve the Outer Gods, and many with more horrific powers than her. Ultimately, Starry

Wisdom wants one of the Outer Gods ruling the human realm. That would not be a good thing, sweetling."

I heaved out a sigh at his understatement. After draining my beer and our depressing chat, I felt bone tired. I couldn't take more tonight. "Okay, look. We have to talk about this—me, Gareth, and Harley. You have a phone or anything?"

"No," he said, eyeing me, "though I will acquire one soon. I will stop by Warm Regards in two days, yes? We can then discuss your decision."

"Fine by me." I stood to leave. "Thanks for the drink," I said, my Midwestern politeness making it impossible for me not to say something.

"My pleasure," he said, snatching my hand in his lightning quick, and placed a gentle kiss on its back. "Anything you desire."

Gareth shifted at my side as I tamped down the liquid fire running through my veins at his touch. "Two days." I nodded and left. I felt Nyarlathotep's eyes on me through the bar, even outside, as I walked back to my place with Gareth in tow.

Gareth was not happy about a lot of things connected with the Outer God, but he was a smart man. "He's a valuable asset to us, if what he says is true," he said after our own private chat outside Warm Regards. He followed me up to my apartment without me asking outright. I didn't want sex, but he'd almost died. I'd fought evil for the first time. A snuggle in bed was in order, especially since I knew I'd get little sleep.

Too much had happened, too much was still up in the air. Lack of sleep sucked, but big, burly, oddly calming librarian arms might help make the experience slightly better.

# TWO

A GOOD NIGHT'S SLEEP hadn't come. I got a solid four hours, so I guess that counted as at least half of a good night's sleep. The next morning, I was definitely dragging. Yasmiin's skills with the espresso machine perked me up a little. As did Gareth's sweet but heated good-bye kiss before he went off to do library or mage things. I wasn't flying high but was feeling solid, until Harley called and asked me to ride over to the Starry Wisdom spot with her. She was right. It was a good call to double-check everything after the battle. I still grumbled when I agreed.

I slipped into her car when she pulled into my back lot right at 2:00 p.m. and gave a gruff "What's up?" I got a chin lift and silence in return, so I slouched in the seat and closed my eyes behind my sunglasses. Early summer in Ohio was beautiful, sunny and warm without the humidity that would eventually make walking anywhere outside for over thirty seconds a sticky mess. With my tired eyes and grumpy mood I didn't appreciate it, so I hid from it as best I could.

Eventually Harley waded into the silence. "What did you learn from Nyarlathotep?"

"We'll probably find more than we want to find on our little excursion."

She didn't take her eyes off the road or speak, but she arched her thick black eyebrow in question, so I gave her a basic rundown of what he'd said at the bar. He needed us to Nancy Drew with him, and we probably would also need his help if another Outer God was in the mix. All to avoid death and destruction. Basic Friday afternoon conversation.

Harley muttered some colorful expletives to herself, sounding as tired and annoyed as I felt, though I have to say her outward appearance held up better. She wore her standard uniform: crisp slacks well molded to her body and a sharp yet colorful button-up shirt pushed up to her elbows. Her tight black curls sat close to her head, and her dark-brown skin reflected the shifting tones of shadow and sun as we drove through the tree-lined streets of Upper Arlington.

She said nothing in reply until we parked several blocks from where the black church once loomed. When she turned off the car, she turned to me and said, "I don't like this."

"Join the club."

"I don't like this," she said again, not missing a beat, "but having an Outer God on our side, even one who isn't at his full power, could be good for us. Especially if the cult isn't gone."

She paused, looking me up and down, before she said in her usual blunt manner, "It'd be best for you too."

"How?"

"It's clear I can't help you a whole lot with your specific brand of magic."

"You hold your own," I said, not wanting her to think she didn't help me.

"I'm an excellent mage with exceptional power and skill," she said. It wasn't bragging from her, simply facts. I thought back to the power she'd called and wielded last night. It had been awe-inspiring, even to someone new to all this magic business. "Still. I can't fully understand what you need because you're not a mage. You're something else."

"Yay," I said sarcastically. I may have even thrown up some jazz hands for emphasis.

"It's not good or bad, Randy. It's simple fact. You're something different, and I don't have all the knowledge you might need. Don't get it twisted. I have a lot, but I don't have all the answers or connections to some of your powers. Particularly the shadow powers you wield, your dream walking, and any number of other things you haven't even discovered inside yourself yet."

I finished her thought for her. "The Outer God supposedly does."

"Yeah." She turned back to look out the windshield, then said, "This doesn't mean we won't work together, explore magic together. Means we add another person to our roster."

"I liked our team of five. Like a basketball team on the court. Five's a good number."

"Any good ball team needs a deep bench, Randy, and Nyarlathotep is as deep as it gets."

"You think we can trust him?" I asked.

"No, or at least not yet. I think we can have what you and I had at the beginning, a mutually beneficial arrangement."

"You don't think we have an agreement anymore?"

"I'd say we have more."

I gasped in mock outrage. "Harley. Are we actually friends now?"

She shrugged. "You fight an evil cult with a person, things change. Plus, Merry and I are tight now."

"Oh, I see. You're saying all this just to stay in good with my sister," I said teasingly.

"Merry and I are solid," she answered, a soft smile hitting her face for the second she said my sister's name. "Doesn't mean you and I aren't also solid, in a different way."

I respected the hell out of Harley and liked her with my sister. Liked her. Made my heart squeeze a little to hear her say something similar. I answered, "Same."

"Good. Now let's get down to business," Harley called as she opened her door and stretched her lean body out of the car. I scurried behind her, hoping we'd find nothing but an empty clearing when we made it to the cult site again.

OF COURSE, NO SUCH luck. I watched, slack jawed, as men in large 4x4 trucks rolled out of the hidden lane, hauling huge loads of beams—the intricately carved wood of the shelter house where Starry Wisdom had tried to kidnap me.

I was about to say it might have been a regular demo crew when a tiny red convertible rolled to a stop at the mouth of the entrance. The woman behind the wheel wore huge black sunglasses and a blue polka-dot scarf wrapped around her from the neck up, hiding her hair. But it was Macy. For sure Macy.

I gave a frustrated huff and said, "You've got to be shitting me."

"Looks like she escaped the shadow world," Harley mumbled.

I seethed at Harley's side, unable to respond from the rage boiling in my blood. She'd made serious threats to me and those I loved last night, and to see her here and now was too much. I whirled from our spot, crouched behind a large bush, and stalked away, my fists clenched and shaking. DD shook as hard out of the corner of my eye. For a second, I thought about sending it out like a bullet, making it ricochet through the tiny car, through Macy, until there was nothing left of either. The sunshine didn't match my dark thoughts, and as much as I hated Macy still kicking around in

our world, I was frightened of the terrible violence I
wanted to unleash on her. Last night, before the battle,
I'd hedged about the possibility of killing. Now I was
apparently jumping to it automatically. I didn't want
to think about what my train of thought might reveal
about me, so I shook off the thoughts as best I could,
but not the worry. Worry was a hard, hot stone in my
chest, driving me back to Harley, the ultimate planner.

She'd waited patiently for my return. "Want to talk
about it?"

"We need more wards for everyone. More protection
charms, if possible. Especially for Merry and Mia," I
said, avoiding the question and getting to more prac-
tical concerns.

"On it," Harley answered with a firm nod. "Merry's
been spending a lot of time at my place, so convincing
her to stay for a prolonged period might not be hard."

"Is this where I make a U-Haul joke?" I quipped,
the anger easing when I thought about my sister happy
and, above all, safe in Harley's heavily warded condo.

Harley simply stared at me a beat, not amused, then
went on. "I doubt Mia will want to leave her place."

"Highly unlikely. It's all tricked out with her favorite
gadgets."

"Then we'll focus there. Me, you, and Gareth can
ward. I'll look into more intricate personal charms
of protection if you want, but short of tattoos, I
don't know anything more effective than the bracelets
Gareth gave you."

I nodded and, making sure no more vehicles or stray cultists were about, turned to go back toward Harley's car. When we'd walked for a couple of minutes, I looked at Harley at my side as she said, "At least we now know Nyarlathotep wasn't lying."

Cold comfort, that was. "What do we do now?"

"It sucks to say it, but we're back at square one. We don't know where the cult will pop up next. If they're staying in Columbus or not. Who's really pulling their strings, if all of what Nyarlathotep said is to be believed."

"They're not leaving Columbus." I don't know how, but I knew it to be true, deep down in my bones—or maybe my shadows. Macy wasn't done here, and if she wasn't exactly the leader, then whoever it was also wasn't done in my town.

"Hope for the best, prepare for the worst," Harley muttered. When the car was in sight, she said, "You need to contact Nyarlathotep. Confirm we will work with him. Also get him to agree to train you in your natural abilities. You focus your attention there. I'll keep track of Starry Wisdom. Or, really, Mia will, and I'll keep on top of what she finds."

"It starts all over again," I said, dejected.

"Starts again, but not at the same point. We're smarter, tougher, stronger, and we now have an Outer God up our sleeve," Harley asserted with a hard voice as she beeped the car to unlock.

Maybe. Possibly. All of it left me feeling discouraged and scared. Scared of what we'd need to do to make it all end once and for all. Scared of what working with Nyarlathotep might do to me, of what my powers might be capable of doing. Above all, scared we'd fail and everyone I loved would be destroyed by monsters—figurative and literal. Once again, average, run-of-the-mill sunny Friday afternoon thoughts.

# THREE

NYARLATHOTEP CAME BY WARM Regards two mornings later, as promised, oozing charm, and a part of me wished his wasn't so charming, or, at least, the charm wasn't pointed my way. Same with those endless starry eyes of his.

He only stayed long enough for me to tell him we would work with him and to ask him to meet me later, somewhere outside my café, to talk magic more in depth. He seemed eager for the meet, which sent a thrill of anticipation and apprehension through me. Lucky for me and my internal resolve to keep at least a little distance from the Prince, he'd gotten a cell. Meant I didn't have to communicate in person all the time... didn't have to feel the zap and sizzle of magic whenever I needed to talk basic logistics.

Later in the afternoon, he texted to ask me to meet him at an address on Olentangy River Road around dusk. As I needed help, and I'd honestly finished my baking and business admin, I agreed. I'd wanted to veg on my couch and zone out with some reality television, something of the home-renovation variety, but I knew this was more important. HGTV streaming was always around; Outer Gods weren't.

When I copied and pasted the address into Maps, I groaned out loud. I shouldn't've been surprised. Where else would a goth-like Outer God, Prince of the Dreamlands, want to meet up but a cemetery? The initial creep factor skeeved me enough I wanted to give the god a piece of my mind when I saw him.

I turned off Olentangy at the large brick pillar marking Union Cemetery. The summer sun was hitting the horizon, not quite setting but barreling close to it. It blazed a deep orange red, glaring in my eyes and blurring my vision for a split second, so I was startled when what I thought was an empty lane past an open black metal gate was actually filled with a smiling deity.

I slammed the brakes quickly, coming within inches of Nyarlathotep. He didn't move. Didn't even flinch. Stood straight and tall in the leathers he refused to change, sexy smile on his lips, heat in his night eyes, the summer sun making his sandy skin glisten slightly.

I shook off the heightened sensation of my thrum connecting with whatever was inside him and sent him a scowl. He laughed and slowly walked to my passenger door. Surprisingly, he didn't open it right away. He gestured toward the handle as he looked at me, silently asking for permission before he got into my tiny car.

It was unnecessary, for him at least. He had the power to go anywhere, do practically anything, in my world. Yet he stopped and asked, though not in words. My heart softened a touch at the gesture, the acknowledgment of me and what I may or may not want, the proof he was willing to listen and do, depending on my needs.

I flung my head to the side, a flippant come-on-then gesture hiding how much his action affected me and my perception of him. He smiled with full teeth, teeth that looked a touch too sharp in his mouth, which sent my nerves back into overdrive.

As he slid into my car, he said, "Thank you for meeting me, sweetling."

"Randy." I eased down the paved cemetery lane as I spoke.

"As you wish, Randy," he said, elongating my name, teasing the word with his tongue so it somehow sounded decadent and obscene. This guy was walking, talking sexiness. I needed none of it from him, so I ignored it as best I could.

"Where to?"

"Anywhere on the grounds will serve our purpose," he answered with a shrug, though his eyes stayed glued to my profile. I looked ahead, seeing DD quiver with anticipation on one side of me, Nyarlathotep giving me an intense, evaluative stare on the other. I felt caught between two types of darkness: one I was coming to know well, the other fathomless on some level.

"No wish to see Dave Thomas or Woody Hayes then?" I asked to try to ease some of my own tension.

"No wish to see anyone but you, Randy," he purred in reply, too quick for my liking and too attentive and focused on me, as usual.

Like a big dork, I said, "Righty-ho," as I pulled the car over off a side lane in the cemetery, wanting out of the confined space, hoping for a little less tension, a little less thrum of magic between us. It made me feel on edge, mainly because I didn't know anything about Nyarlathotep except it would be stupid to fully trust him. I lusted after him, sure, but I also got zaps of lust from Gareth, and he was a solid dude I didn't have to worry about too much. A better choice. A safer choice. However, a little voice in the back of my mind asked what might happen if I made a different choice. Or, maybe, why I needed to choose at all.

Tamping the voice down, I looked around us. Rows of staggered headstones stretched out all around. Some old, some new, some with flowers and small trinkets, some ignored or abandoned through time. Sweeping my arm out, I asked, "What's this all about? The cemetery will close pretty soon, you know."

"At dark, yes. We're here for dusk."

"Why?"

He stalked closer, as calm and lithe as the lion I'd first met. Likely as dangerous, in more ways than one. He stopped inches from my body, though I felt the heat and magic of him rubbing along my skin. "Because I suspect, like me, you are a creature of the inbetween.

We start in a place inbetween at a time inbetween to test my assumptions."

I had nothing to add, so I stared back, waiting. He inclined his head at DD, clearly able to see it. DD shivered even harder, filled with pent-up excitement. "You have a chunk of Deep Dark at heel, I see."

"DD and I work well together."

"DD." He laughed. "Like your pet? For you, may not be too far off. I imagine it does your bidding well."

"When it's needed."

"What else have you done, Randy?"

"I've performed spells, slipped into shadows, walked in the shadow world... Oh, and I've dream walked too. That's about it."

"Impressive," he said, sincerity clear in his voice, which made me stand a little straighter. Not every day I impressed an Outer God. "Have you called on shades?"

"Shades?"

"What you humans like to call the spirits of the dead. Not quite, but close enough. The energy left behind when certain humans die is more accurate."

"You want me to speak to ghosts? Go all *Sixth Sense*?" I asked, taking a small step backward as if the very idea of it literally bowled me over. "I'd rather not, but thanks."

"There is nothing to fear, Randy." He took my hand in his.

The zap of power and lust I felt made my legs wobble, but I turned with him easily. My magic thrummed to life, ready and willing to do whatever Nyarlathotep asked, which was overwhelming and dangerous in equal measure.

He scented the air beside me, like I'd seen his black lion form do, and his head whipped to me quickly, almost too quickly, making his eyes reflect the dying light in an animalistic flash of green. It took my breath for a moment, seeing the mix of human and lion in one. Being reminded, yet again in a span of a few minutes, he was something else, something other. Something dangerous my magic and my body wanted, despite of or because of the danger.

"It's close. These inbetween times in the human plane make my skin tingle. Dusk. Dawn. Perfect transitory elements for working our brand of magic."

"How are you so certain it's 'our' brand of magic?" I asked. Partially to be contrary and stave off the complex emotions he brought up. Partially to honestly understand the answer.

"Because the Book of Knowing told me so," he answered blandly before his voice heated, lowered, and became something more feral. "Because I feel you inside of me."

I nodded and stared at his beautiful face. How was I even supposed to reply? No way I could, without lying or revealing too much, so I kept my trap shut.

He moved on without saying more. "Let us try, then, to see the shades together."

He instructed me to close my eyes, to listen to the thrum of magic, and tune it into my intention. "It is a frequency, so to speak. Your magic can do many things, but it must adjust to each, based on your will and desire."

I followed his instructions, thought of what I wanted, and felt an answer in my core, a sort of call-and-response from me to my magic. After a few minutes of me stoking my magic, asking and receiving in vibes only, he told me to open my eyes.

When I did, I saw them, small wisps of beings who had definitely not been in the cemetery before. More likely I'd not been able to see them before because I wasn't looking hard enough. A handful, maybe six total, wandered the gravesite in front of me, aimless and looking far less concerned than I would have imagined.

"Don't they want anything? Ghosts have a reason to stay behind, right?"

"Not necessarily. If a human's will is strong enough, yes. If they have excess energy from other means, natural and supernatural, they become shades, echoes of what they were. Beings in another form once again waiting to move on to the next form they will eventually take."

"Energy never dies. It changes," I whispered, one of the few things I remembered from my honors physics class in high school.

"Too true," he said, squeezing the hand he still held. "Enough for here and now. Call down your magic."

He gave me instructions on how to adjust my thrum to an active background element using will and intention once again. My magic responded, turning into a steady thump in the background of my mind, not as jarring as it had been since I'd noticed it after my little vision quest but not gone either.

"Thank you, Nyarlathotep," I said, genuinely grateful for what he'd given me in so short a time. The shade business wasn't something I wanted—I didn't imagine I'd ever use it—but being able to successfully control the magic inside myself with a simple switch in my thinking amazed me.

"Ny, please. Much like you, I prefer the shorter version."

It made me laugh, the all-too-human desire to name oneself. "Okay, Ny. Will do."

I had to know something though, before any more lessons could go on. Getting to the something was hard for me. I circled the issue instead. "Why couldn't Harley or Gareth teach me that?" I asked.

"They didn't know. Both Harley and Gareth hold tremendous skill, knowledge, and potential. Harley especially can hold and wield immense power, given what I felt from her in the black church. Yet they are mages. They do not have their own magic inside of themselves. You and I do. We contain a well of magic. We don't need to wrestle it from the earth or other sources. Our magic is something unique, tied to our very beings. It may seem a small distinction, but it is an important one."

Made sense. Mages needed to pull and store magic. I didn't have to because I had a thrum of magic on tap somehow. The somehow was the sticking point for me.

"Why do I have this well of magic thing? I'm just a human."

"Why is the grass green and the sky blue here? It simply is, and we are happy for it to be so."

I scoffed. "Okay, Socrates."

"A thoughtful human indeed, but don't dismiss my point, Randy." He stepped even closer, our joined hands pulled up and crushed between us, the one thing keeping our chests from touching. "I cannot answer why you are as you are. Do not know who could. All I can say is I am happy you are, as are all in your circle. I saw it clearly in your café. I hope you are also. Can't that be enough?"

I blushed and, instead of answering, stared down at our joined hands, our rising and falling chests. I wanted to say yes. Say he was kind for saying it, for being happy I was who I was, because it was maybe the sweetest thing any person had ever said to me. But I couldn't. There was this question hovering over me, this idea I was more than I seemed, that I was meant for something else. Like a nagging sense another shoe was waiting to drop. Until it did, I could be happy about a lot of things, but I couldn't celebrate what I might be.

# Four

I DIDN'T EVEN GET forty-eight hours to sort out my feelings about my first lesson with Ny before more magical crap hit the proverbial fan. It came in a surprising form at least: a text from Merry asking me to meet her at Harley's.

She'd texted me previously about a potential lead for a baking assistant, someone I desperately needed at this point, as wedding cupcake season was in full swing. I was baking well into the night, on top of getting as much magic study and training in on my own as I could without an anchor, on top of meeting with Harley and Gareth and now Ny, on top of trying to have some semblance of a social life. Guess which one suffered?

My café staff was great. All squared away and run by the always-on-top-of-things Deb. I couldn't keep up with the demand in the café and in special orders. I was drowning, and the life-preserver was a baking assistant who could start ASAP. In fact, I'd been in such a rush the other day, I'd snagged the ward-protection-bracelet-thingy Gareth gave me on the corner of a hot baking sheet. A sheet so hot, it snapped the thing. Felt bad about it, but it had been an accident. I'd have to tell him and beg for another one.

Luckily for me, Merry was on top of the business end of things, had done her number crunching, and based on her projections put out feelers for potential candidates. She knew a lot of people because of her non-profit work, so she was always a good person to call on when looking to hire. She was on the case, looking for someone to help bake tasty treats while I dealt with evil cults and magic mess.

When I arrived at Harley's in the evening, exhausted and smelling of orange-bun frosting, I thought she'd found me someone cool to help ease the baking load.

Harley opened the door without a word, simply stepping aside to let me enter. I hung back in her foyer so she could walk past. I realized I'd never been anywhere in Harley's condo other than the office we used as a fight pad, and I didn't know if our meeting about bakers would take place there. However, she strolled in her usual manner right to the hallway door leading to the floor below. Maybe she didn't like too many guests in the rest of her house.

When I entered the open space on the second level, I found my sister curled up in Harley's comfy reading chair. Her head was bent over a heavy book so her thick, dark hair shrouded her face from view, and her slender legs were hidden somewhere under her flowy white dress. It gave the illusion she hovered rather than sat; a slim, floating figure out of some dark Gothic tale. The vision shattered when she noticed my arrival. Her head lifted at the sound of my sneakers squeaking across the high-polished floor and she looked at me with bright, happy brown eyes and a wide, open smile. No more ghostly apparition, just plain old pretty Merry.

"Randy," she called, folding herself out of the chair to grab me in a solid one-armed hug. Her other arm held the large book close to her side with a finger marking her page.

"You look mighty comfy here, Merry," I drawled, my eyes bouncing between her smiling face, a face I knew as well as my own, and Harley's tall, dark figure, now leaning against her desk. No one else spoke, so after a few seconds, I continued. "So, what brings me here? Please tell me you've found me a baking assistant."

Merry's eyes rounded. "Oh, no. Sorry. I have a lead, a really good lead, but I need to talk to the person first. Then I'll send them your way, okay?"

I nodded and waited. Merry said nothing. Harley stared at her before wading into the silence. "Your sister has been doing some research in my study."

"Research? Like magical-mage type research? Why?"

"Well, Mia's been doing her online thing, and everyone else has some power or whatever. I wanted to help out more. Figured I'd do a little reading into a particular problem."

"The problem of you lacking an anchor," Harley said.

I opened my mouth, annoyed by this turn of events, but Harley cut me off.

"Don't even start. I didn't ask her to do it, and I don't like she did it. Found her down here one night, and she told me what she was looking for. Once I knew I couldn't stop her, I steered her away from the more arcane reading and set her up with a few things she could easily dig into. She actually found something."

DD thumped in excitement at my side. Apparently one of us was very happy I'd have some help in my dreams.

"Don't sound so surprised," Merry said with a pout.

"Not surprised at you finding something, hon. Surprised there was anything to find. That's all," Harley said with a soft tone I rarely heard from her. Merry smiled broadly back, and the crackle between them was enough to make me blush. Yeah, their relationship was definitely solid now.

"Okay. Not liking it, but I know you're stubborn as hell," I said to Merry.

"Same, sis," she replied, before pulling the large book back up to leaf through. "In this instance, a helpful stubborn. I found something, a joining spell where you can also create an anchor. Ran it by Harley, and she agrees it will work in our situation."

"What do you mean 'our situation,'" I said slowly, liking this less and less as the conversation went on.

"Our. As in you and me. You'll use me as your anchor," Merry answered, her voice and face showing she was all kinds of eager.

"Nope. No way. Not happening." I said, slashing my hand down and using my best firm big-sister voice. "Don't care what it entails, how it works. There's no way I'm using you."

"It's not using if I understand what I'm getting into and agree to do it."

Harley stepped into the fray. "Randy, I know it sounds bad. Believe me, I didn't like the idea at first either." She slid her gaze up and down Merry. "Your sister is very persuasive, and the magic isn't actually too difficult or demanding for anyone involved."

"Wait. You told me before it was a long, complicated process to get an anchor."

"It is, when you're creating one from an object or space. However, Merry found a way to join two people already emotionally connected, join them in a way it creates an anchor for each."

"Since we're already bonded, the magic is easier to perform and less likely to do harm," Merry said.

"You can't know," I said with the shake of my head. "And you." I pinned Harley with a stare. "You should know better."

"All magic is volatile in some way, sure," Harley answered with a shrug. "This, though, is easy magic.

Something I should have thought of myself if I hadn't been so focused on making an inanimate anchor point for you. It's somewhat embarrassing I didn't think of this before. I'd been considering ways to make Warm Regards your anchor. This is so much easier."

She pushed herself off the desk and got close. "You have to know I wouldn't have agreed without looking into it myself and knowing it would be safe for her."

I hung my head. Dammit, she was right. No way, with how Harley and Merry were going, she'd do anything that might harm my sister. I still didn't want my sister wrapped up in this.

"Randy, please," Merry said, a hint of sadness in her voice tugging at my heart. "Everyone else has some big role to play in this. Let me help you where I can."

"Isn't being an awesome sister enough of a role?"

She smiled. "I'll be your awesome sister and your anchor."

Her dark eyes were determined but loving, and I knew she'd latch onto this and never let go, never let up, until I agreed.

DD, who'd been jumping a little too excitedly near the corner of my eye, swooped in, close to my face, and gave me an encouraging swipe on my cheek. Another vote yes from the ball of darkness.

Turning to Harley, I asked, "You're positive this won't hurt her?"

"She might get a headache every now and then, when she has to help pull you through something. She'll also be able to sense when you're in danger or afraid, which will cause her own fear and anxiety to spike, but she'll remain safe and grounded wherever she is, creating a type of warning system either of you can access when you feel the need."

I cut a side-eye back at my sister, who looked ready to burst with excitement. She wanted this. I needed this. If I was honest, we all might need this if it allowed me to explore my own powers more on my own, grow and change so I could offer more solid protection. I gave an exaggerated sigh to let everyone in the room know my supreme level of annoyance and muttered, "Fine. How're we going to do this?"

MERRY AND I SAT criss-cross applesauce across from each other, the points of our knees slightly touching. First, I had to push DD away. It acted all hangdog about it, but it was supposedly better to do this spell without anything else connected to the participants at the moment. I did promise I'd call it back immediately.

Harley settled herself between us but outside our circle, then explained again what she would do. "I'll cast the spell, with the help of the sigil circle you two are sitting on right now. It will do a number of things in rapid order: pull both of you into your subconscious selves, create some type of bridge between your consciousnesses, and join you together. It's a basic joining spell. The end result is a two-way anchor of sorts, though I doubt Merry will ever use her end. After this, you'll be psychically linked."

"Like twinsies," Merry said with a laugh.

"Not a bad comparison, the twin bond. Your connection should flare when one of you is feeling a heightened negative emotion or makes a concerted effort to tug on the connection."

It all made sense, seemed so simple, and I believed Harley's multiple assurances. I still wasn't happy about it, so I grumbled and said, "If we're doing this, let's get it over with."

Merry and Harley ignored my grumpiness. My sister closed her eyes, breathed deep, and relaxed herself, more than ready to do this monumental thing for me. Harley watched her with admiration and care oozing out of her face, enough to make me ratchet my annoyance down a few pegs. She turned to me after a beat and raised her dark, slashing eyebrows my way. I shrugged and followed Merry's lead, closing my eyes and trying to relax myself, body and mind, the best I could.

Harley's strong voice began a complicated chant I didn't even try to follow. After a few lines, I felt a tingle start in my body. Oddly, it started in my butt. Really, it wasn't too odd as I focused on it. The tingle began in the spot where my body literally touched the sigil circle, spreading out slowly, out and up, until it eventually made its way to the tip-top of my head. When my skull felt like it was buzzing, a fireworks show started behind my eyes.

Gold sparks scattered in the dark, showering without any pattern I could pick out, almost like children frantically zipping sparklers around in the darkness with no rhyme or reason to their movements. Slowly, they began to pulse in tune with my heartbeat, a thump I could see and feel. The pulsing golden sparks then moved together, joining, becoming one bright golden mass before it blinked out and roared back to life in a tangible shape.

In my mind, my hand reached out to touch the thing now hovering in the black. It was an old telephone with a long, curly cord connecting the base with the headset. It looked identical to the one we had in our kitchen growing up, except this one was made from glistening gold rather than cheap plastic.

I took hold of the handle, put it to my ear, and listened. No dial tone. Instead, I heard a tinkle of vivid laughter. "Hey, Randy," Merry said down the line, her voice taking on the weird echo I vaguely remembered from landline phones in the 1990s.

"Merry, Merry, quite contrary." I laughed, my mind racing through images of us playing as girls in our old kitchen, teasing and running and laughing, filled with love almost to bursting. The emotions blossomed, swelled out, made my voice and Merry's voice stronger as we both laughed together down the line.

"I'm hanging up now," I finally said.

"Pick up the phone whenever you need, Randy," she called back in reply, her voice insistent though still tinged with our laughter, our love.

"I will," I whispered, hanging the phone back on the cradle and blinking my eyes in Harley's condo. When I was once again outside my mind, I felt the tears of joy that had gathered there.

I shook out my head and looked across from me to see Merry's brilliant, smiling face—a face I knew better than my own, one I'd watched grow from infancy into womanhood—and I shook off any apprehension I'd ever had about this anchor business.

"I love you," I said.

"Right back atcha," she said with a rough warmth in her voice.

We reached out to hold each other, happy and safe and not newly joined. We'd always been joined. Now there was something in our heads that gave the connection immediate access and voice. A new form for an old, steady love.

# FIVE

I WAS WARM AND fuzzy for a few days after Merry became my anchor. DD was hyped too, especially once I brought it back to me as promised. It stayed close from then on, coming in and out of sight, ready and around in case I needed it.

The chat with Mia about Merry becoming my anchor doused the fuzzies some. Made me feel a little bad my youngest sister wasn't in the mix, though she didn't seem concerned. She was far more concerned about some book she wanted to talk with me about. She insisted Gareth be there too.

Gareth and I were solid. We had had little time since the events at the black church to connect in person, what with our own jobs and magical research going down at the same time, but we'd flirted relentlessly via text. His sexting game was on point.

Mia asking for a meeting with both of us was odd but gave me an excuse to call Gareth over to my house. Hopefully the news wouldn't be so devastating I'd forget all about wanting to play out some of the more explicit text exchanges we'd had over the course of the past few days. With Mia and her idea of shenanigans skirting the lines of the legal and the intelligent, I wouldn't hold my breath.

It was a sunny Thursday evening around seven when Mia breezed into my apartment without knocking. She eyed me up and down and quirked an eyebrow at me in silent judgment of my look. Mia knew usual-evening Randy was all about comfy pajama pants and old T-shirts, hair up in a messy bun. This evening I was in skinny jeans, a low V-neck black tee that molded nicely to my full body, and a smattering of makeup. My black hair was down and gleaming. There was lip gloss in the mix but no lipstick. I didn't want my delicious plans for later bungled by smearing maroon all over the place.

"Don't hate the player," I said jokingly, and Mia snorted at my ridiculous line. For her part, she looked put together in her usual way, short dark hair in a slick style, her petite and curvy 1930s ingenue build somehow highlighted by the simple T-shirt and jeans she wore. Her brown eyes were assessing behind those black-rimmed glasses of hers.

"Whatever. I take it Gareth has yet to show?"

"You're a little early. Unlike some people, Gareth announces himself and waits for an invitation into my home."

"Take my keys then," she said, unconcerned. No way I was taking away her access to my place, and she damn well knew it.

I grumbled wordlessly but the drone of a motorcycle caught my attention. Gareth's motorcycle, I guessed, as two minutes later someone rang my downstairs doorbell.

Mia absently waved me on as she set up her laptop on my kitchen counter, her concentration face in full effect.

I may have run down the stairs, been a little breathless when I opened the door wide to see Gareth there, a soft smile on his lush lips. His beard was a little scraggly, like he'd had no time to trim, but I liked it that way. He eyed me, though it was nothing like how Mia had. It was searing heat, his gaze a physical thing as it moved from my dark head to my black-painted toes.

Pulling him to me without a word, I stretched up on those toes to reach his mouth and landed a hot, hard kiss there. Gareth took it and deepened it, banding an arm around my back to move me into his strong body, surround me with his scent and muscles as his insistent lips pushed me back into an arch. I moaned softly and he ate it up, literally nibbling my lips before thrusting his tongue deep into my mouth.

We stayed clenched in our intense kiss for long minutes. I was panting by the time he disconnected. He didn't go far, resting his forehead on my own. Our eyes—navy to hazel—met, and his held clear desire and want. "Hello, Randy," he said, the first words spoken in our minutes together a deep rumble sounding from his chest.

"Hey, big guy," I whispered, smiling brightly as I went back to the bare soles of my feet, separating us farther. Hopefully not for much longer.

His gaze shifted to my arm, then he pulled it down from around his neck, looking right at my now-empty wrist.

"I was going to tell you," I said. "I was busy, rushing, and accidently snapped it in the kitchen the other day. Probably shouldn't have even had it on in the kitchen, but live and learn, I guess. I'm sorry."

"Accidents happen," he answered with a shrug. "I do worry you're running around without the protection."

"I know you're busy and all, but could you make me another one?"

"Definitely, but it takes time, Randy. Because of your magic, the wards require more work. They must be tuned to you specifically."

I cocked my head at the new info. "How long?"

"At least a month and a half, so I'll start right away."

I gave a sexy smile. "You were so into me, Gareth. Making special bracelets for me before we even did it."

He didn't verbally answer, simply stared down at me, gripped my hip tight, and gave it a slow caress. It sent a shiver to my lady bits.

He shook himself free of the lust now curling around us. "Know what this is about yet?" he said, flicking his head in the direction of my upstairs apartment, the direction of Mia.

"Nope," I said with a pop, "but we're about to find out." Sliding my hands down from his shoulders, I took one of his and led the way upstairs.

"Thought you two might take longer," Mia said teasingly as we entered the apartment, though she didn't take her eyes off her laptop screen.

I ignored the jab and instead asked, "Snacks?" as I pulled a plate of rose and pistachio shortbread cookies out of a cabinet. If I hadn't put them away, Mia would've descended on them as soon as she came into the place.

Without a word, Mia grabbed for the plate, taking three of the squares at once, though thankfully she only shoved one in her mouth. "Thanks, sis," she said, her full mouth covered by her hand to maintain at least some semblance of decorum.

I laughed and turned to Gareth, who took one, giving a chin lift in thanks. "Even vegan. Made with tasty vegan butter, applesauce instead of eggs, and almond milk in the powdered sugar icing," I said for no reason in particular except I wanted to let them know.

"Vegan cookies and yummy to boot? These going on the menu?" Mia asked, stuffing another in her face.

"For the summer, yeah."

Nodding, she whipped out her phone to take a few shots of the last cookie in her hand. "Awesome. I'll fancy these pics up in Photoshop later and post them. People will come running for sure."

I thanked her and grabbed my own cookie, then took it down in a few crumbly, sweet, floral bites. Wiping down my hands and the counter with my ever-present kitchen towel, I said, "Okay, kid. Spill it. What's so important you need both me and Gareth here?"

Gareth stood by me, silent but leaning gently against my side. Mia looked between us then started. "I asked for Gareth rather than Harley because I know he specializes in occult texts in his library gig."

Both Gareth and I raised eyebrows at this. Me because he'd never told me his specialty, though it made sense given he was a mage who worked as a special collections librarian at a university. Gareth likely because he didn't realize Mia knew so much about him. Didn't surprise me. My little sister was nosy and had a way around supposedly safe information stored online.

Gareth didn't interject, so I motioned for Mia to get to the point.

"Yeah, so ever since Harley asked for Starry Wisdom research, I've been poking my head into some odd corners of the internet—odd even by my quirky internet standards. I noted reference to a particular book a few times, online whispers about what it might be able to do. No one seemed to have a full copy anymore, the last mostly complete copy being stolen from some stuffy New England university forever ago. Despite the ghosting, in certain circles, everyone still talked about it."

"What's this book?" I asked, still not seeing the connection.

"The Necronomicon?" Gareth guessed.

"Bingo, my man." Turning to explain it to me, Mia said, "The tale goes like this. There was this guy named Abdul Alhazred, a poet and mystic from Yemen way back in the day. He apparently wandered far out into the desert and found something—something that made his magics stronger and gave him vast knowledge of the mystical worlds, but something that also stalked him out of the desert, according to the chatter about him at the time, or at least whatever was passed all the way down to us. He wrote what he discovered in a book he called Kitab Al-Azif, what most today who know of it call the Necronomicon. He did all this in around the year seven thirty, then stayed hidden for a long time. People said he ended up shredded by some invisible monster in the streets of Damascus in seven thirty-eight, according to eye-witness accounts of what seems to be a damn gruesome death."

"Not sounding good, Mia," I muttered. A shiver went up my spine as I thought about the types of monsters that I knew couldn't be seen in our plane but roamed freely in others, like the shadow world.

"Let me get to the good stuff, Randy," Mia answered. "The Arabic was translated into Greek, then Latin, then the European languages. Then it was sullied or destroyed or outright burned in the streets for the magic it discussed and the spells it held. One final, supposedly full, text in English, thought to be translated by the famous Elizabethan mystic John Dee, was displayed at a New England university for decades before it disappeared one night. Some say it was outright destroyed, others say it was ripped apart, piece by piece, and scattered in a way no one could put it back together. As of today, a few fragmented texts remain, and those are locked away—by occult collectors or deep in university libraries." With the last line, Mia looked right at Gareth.

"Ohio State does not have a copy of the Necronomicon," he said in reply to her stare.

"Oh, I know, but I suspect you have access to some parts of a copy. Somewhere."

"Why obsessively go on and on about this? All you've told me about is a sketchy book, which isn't especially helpful right now."

"Beyond the basic magic power and insight it holds," Mia said, "the book supposedly has an entire section of a very rare form of magic: shadow magic."

I sucked in a breath and DD made itself known, swooping in my eyesight with a happy little jump. A book that could help me with my specific powers would be nice.

"I've never heard this," Gareth said, "and I've done extensive research on the book."

"There are vague references, but I've found them. I can send you the info."

"What are we supposed to do with this information, Mia?" Gareth asked.

"Find the book for Randy, of course. Get a copy, or as close to a whole copy as we can, and see what's in this extra-special book."

"I've read through several fragments. I know Harley has, too, because we've talked about them at length. None discussed shadow magic."

"I know, but look." She twisted her laptop around to show us a scan of some old English writing. "This is from John Dee himself. He said the book has hidden instructions, only accessible when a whole copy is formed."

"Meaning we need to find a whole copy of an ancient book no one has been able to find for centuries."

"Not necessarily," Mia said with a sly smile. "What's to say it needs to be a whole bound copy?"

"You want to make a digitized whole," Gareth said on a harsh exhale. He cocked his head in thought, his brows furrowed. After a few beats, he nodded and said, "It could work. Books, and the knowledge they hold, have changed in form at various times in human history. Whatever additional magic the contents of the Necronomicon holds may easily transfer from page to digital screen."

"Wait, wait, wait. How dangerous is this?" I asked, always concerned with what my sisters might be getting into, especially in all this magic business.

"The magic is unknown," Gareth answered, "but tracking down the pieces shouldn't be exceedingly dangerous for someone like Mia."

Mia beamed at this, but I shook my head. Mia would have to do her own computer magic to get certain parts, a form of magic far more illegal than my own, and possibly equally as dangerous.

Gareth turned to face me. "I wouldn't put your sister in danger," he said. "There's also a chance this idea of hers will lead nowhere. Not a single person in decades has claimed to have found all the missing pieces of this book. Given all this, I do think it's worth pursuing."

Mia squealed, obviously happy at Gareth's endorsement, but he turned serious eyes on her. "This does not mean you should be reckless. There are many who would like to have the complete Necronomicon in their hands. It's not something to take lightly."

"No, sir," she said with a smirk. "Seriously, though, I understand. I also know it might not lead anywhere, but I want to try." She reached out a hand toward me and I grabbed hold without hesitation. "For you, Randy."

"I don't want or need you to get into trouble over me, Mia."

"Noted. I'll be extra stealthy."

"This is no time to joke," I said in my most stern big-sister voice, which actually did nothing to either of my little sisters unless they knew they needed to back down. "Magic and power go hand-in-hand for some people. We saw that with Starry Wisdom. We all know power makes people do bad shit."

"True, sis. I promise you I'll be careful."

I looked between her and Gareth. I trusted him to not lie to me about this. I trusted Mia to take care of herself, for the most part. I also knew I couldn't really stop her. My little sister was a bloodhound when it came to helping us Carters—singularly focused and intent on her mission. With a sigh, I asked Gareth, "You'll help her?"

Gareth said he would and gave my hand a reassuring squeeze. Looking at Mia, I finally said, "Fine. Cool. Do it, but so we're clear, I'm telling Merry all about this. She can help fuss over you and what you're doing."

Mia shrugged the threat off and smiled. Closing her laptop with a snap, she moved to get her bag off the floor. "Cool cool," she said to me before looking at Gareth. "I'll loop you in on where I am in the search and what my next steps are via email." She didn't ask him for his email because she of course didn't need it. She already knew it. Was possibly even monitoring it.

I gave her a hug at my door. "Not too much, too fast, hear me? This is all new, and what you find might not be all good."

"No worries. Promise."

She waved her hand over her head as she stomped down my stairs, and I waited until she exited into the sunny, warm evening before I shut and locked my door.

# Six

I LEANED AGAINST THE shut door, forehead to wood, with my eyes closed. Gareth stepped up behind me. His touch was tentative at first, a questioning light hand on my shoulder. When I switched my lean and fell into his strong, waiting arms, his hold was firmer, surer.

"You're worried," he whispered.

"No shit," I said, a bit catty but no less true. There was a lot of magic swirling, new players in the game, unknown motives and positions, and all of it new to me and my sisters. I didn't want Mia wrapped up in anything dangerous, but I also recognized I needed all the help I could get. What she did was a need for her, a need to help me. The same need driving me to worry for and try to protect her. The Carter sister triad would forever go around in this circle, needing each other while wanting to shield and protect each other. Look at what Merry had done for me, what Mia was willing to do for me.

All these thoughts raced around in my head, jamming it tight, as Gareth held me close in his arms. After a few silent minutes, he leaned his chin down to rest on the top of my head and whispered, "Want to watch a movie?"

I silently agreed and turned in his arms to give him a big hug. His hold radiated warmth. His body felt firm yet comfortable, his scent enticing, his aura or whatever it was calming me as always. I buried my head into his massive chest and rubbed my face there like a dog rolling around in a favorite scent. It may be a bit much, but it helped in the moment, and Gareth didn't seem to mind. He held me tighter, even.

Blinking up at him, I asked, "*Scream*?"

"As in the movie or the action? If you need to literally scream, go ahead. I'll plug my ears."

I gave a sharp laugh and swatted at the chest I'd been rubbing myself against. "The movie, big guy. Obviously. Though a little screaming could help."

His eyes darkened and his voice dropped when he replied, "There are times I like to hear you scream."

I shivered at the sound and look from him, anticipation firing across my brain. "I definitely want to scream for you. Soon. First, movie and more cookies."

He smiled, easy and light, seemingly happy to do whatever I wanted. Gareth was like that—easy and accommodating. Made me wonder how easy he would be if I told him about the tickle of excitement my magic felt, I felt, when Ny was around. I think he knew, or at least guessed, but I'd never know until we talked about it. Definitely a conversation for a different night, when sister worries weren't weighing, movies weren't waiting to be watched, and the promise in his eyes wasn't so dark and inviting.

WE GOT ALL THE way to the party scene. Right before the climax, which seemed more than fitting. We'd been snuggling on my couch the whole movie, which turned to very light petting, which turned to me openly rubbing his chest under his shirt. Which brought us to the party scene and my need to make my own party.

I whipped my hand from under his shirt, snagged the remote to pause the movie, and quickly turned back to Gareth with my best come-and-get-it stare. "Want to head to the bedroom?"

He smiled, a wicked gleam in his eye. "No desire to stay on the couch again? It could become tradition, horror movie turning into sex on your couch."

I chuckled. "As much fun as a tradition like that could be, I'd like to move into the bedroom."

Without another word, he scooped me up in his arms and rose from the couch in one fluid, superhuman movement. I wasn't easy to carry, but Gareth didn't miss a beat or a step with me. As he carried me the short distance from couch to bed, he kissed me hard and hot, his tongue licking at the inside of my mouth in a delicious rhythm.

I gave a soft yelp and a giggle when I bounced a bit after he thew me gently on the bed. He moved to crawl over me, but I stopped him short. I noticed DD blink out and was happy for it before I took us further.

"No, no, no. Not yet." I pushed his torso up. "Shirt off," I commanded, and he obeyed without hesitation.

"Now you," he said, and I was more than happy to oblige. I even took off my bra and skinny jeans for good measure, leaving the fire-engine red lace hipster panties stretched across my ample hips and ass. When Gareth caught sight of those, his eyes widened a fraction before he heaved out a tense breath. Oh, he for sure liked that.

He moved to join me on the bed, but I stopped him again, pushing him back to the edge of the bed as I crawled toward him. "No, sir. I want to play," I said, gliding my hand up and over his hard abs before moving to unbutton and unzip his jeans.

"Randy," he called, stopping my hand, though I saw the raw hunger in his look. I brushed whatever he was going to say away with the flick of my hand and undid his jeans, shimmying them and his sensible black boxer briefs down enough to pop him free. His hard length bobbed in front of my face a moment, a treat I was so ready to give myself.

He hissed when my lips met the head, and I almost mimicked the sound as the salty heat of his taste hit my mouth. He was a big guy with a big dick, so I took my time. I teased his head, giving soft licks and kisses, before I engulfed it in my mouth and took a few more inches of him down until I hit my throat. I wasn't one for choking, so I used my hands to help the process, gliding and twisting and sucking as I bobbed up and down.

His hands went to my head. Not to force me down or control the moment, but to hold on tight to help himself stay upright. His groans were guttural, fierce, and shot liquid heat straight to my core.

"God, Randy. That's so good. So fucking good."

I gave his head an extra flick of my tongue, an extra suckle. What could I say? I liked praise.

It was several minutes of this, teasing for moments then deep sucking and hand action. I learned what he liked and took him higher and higher. A long, deep moan spilled from his lips and he tugged back on my hair, insistently enough I knew he was getting close.

I popped off his dick with an audible sound, stood on my knees on the bed so we were practically eye to eye, and licked my lips.

He said, "Shit. You're so fucking hot, Randy. I don't want this to end yet."

Gareth shook his head, as if to clear the haze of lust, and pushed me back on the bed. In a flash, he hooked his hands into my panties and tore them down my legs. I was in no position to stop him and didn't want to anyway. I liked playing with him, tasting him, but the pounding in my blood told me I needed him inside me in a different way.

He dropped to the floor on his knees and grabbed my legs to yank me to the edge. "Now I get to play," he growled. He parted my lips with one hand as he lazily dragged a finger from the other up and down my aching center. "So beautiful. So wet. So ready for me," he whispered before he dove right in, hitting my clit with his mouth without hesitation.

My back arched so hard at the flash of pleasure searing my nerves I nearly came off the bed. The vibrations of Gareth's own moan or chuckle, I couldn't tell which, heightened the feeling and he didn't let up. He licked and sucked like a champ, taking me higher and higher. Then his fingers came into the mix. First one, then another dipped deep inside me, hooking up to hit a beautiful spot, making my limbs shake and my breath whoosh from my lungs.

As he did this, he snaked a hand up and across my hips, pressing down on the swell of my lower belly so I felt trapped between his working hands and his tongue, with outward and inner pressure playing off each other. It was an onslaught of wicked sensations. I panted, I moaned, and I may have even shouted incoherently. I didn't know. What I did know is I lasted mere minutes and then exploded, my orgasm a bright flash of fire across and under my skin, causing my body to quake and quiver in its wake.

"Damn, that was good," I finally said after I was able to catch my breath.

Gareth's eyes were hot and hard on me, and without a word, he lifted the fingers he had planted inside me moments before and sucked them into his mouth, groaning around them. "You taste so sweet," he said before he rose up to lie beside me on the bed.

His eyes softened a touch and he reached up to tuck a few stray, and likely very sweaty, dark hairs behind my ear. "Are you okay?"

"More than okay, big guy."

"We can stop now, if you want. I know tonight was a lot for you."

I melted at his words, easing into him and hugging his naked body close to my own. He was so very sweet, so calm and giving. So kind. It made me want to eat him up like one of my cupcakes. It definitely made me want to keep going.

I pulled back quickly. "Nope. I'm not done with you yet," I said as I pulled his big body on top of mine, wanting to feel his weight on me. He smiled and nodded, kissing me deep. I tasted the both of us twined in my mouth, as we'd be twisted together in this bed soon, as life seemed to be pushing us together in so many ways. I wasn't upset about any of it.

GARETH HAD FUCKED ME good and proper. So good and proper, I was ready to pass out. After he got rid of the condom, he slipped under the covers and pulled me tight into his boxer-brief-clad body. I pushed my ass against him, which got me a chuckle in response, before he leaned down to kiss my cheek. "Good night, Randy," he whispered.

"Night, Gareth," I responded, my voice feeling heavy with pleasant post-sexy-times exhaustion. Not much registered after, so I must've fallen into sleep quickly, a first since the events at the black church.

The next thing I knew, I was standing in my long black sleep shirt in front of a busted-up old house. I was dreaming. I knew I was dreaming, but what I didn't know for sure was whether I was dream walking.

The house looked real enough, like it could be somewhere in Columbus. Somewhere in an older part of town because it was a Victorian-esque structure that had seen better days. The two-story house loomed within the confines of a wrought-iron fence. The lawn was overgrown, tall grass swaying slightly as if there was a breeze I couldn't feel. I stood on a cracked front sidewalk leading to a cracked walkway, which led to a set of busted descending stairs. The porch beyond was dark and uninviting. The front door was visible but barely, a once-red color faded from sun and time. The rest of the exterior was various shades of gray, the effect of warping and paint peeling in chunks. Some shutters were on the front, others hung at a slant. One window had no shutters at all.

From the window, a faint flicker of light shone through the darkness. A shadow rushed across it, so quick I couldn't make out exactly what it was. Then, a cackle, hard and sharp like a whip, ripped through the air. The kind of cackle cartoon witches had, which I knew couldn't be good. Especially since the sound made my magic thrum in a not-good way, as if on high alert. Whatever had made it was something I for sure needed to stay away from, even if this was a simple dream.

It was then I noticed DD wasn't anywhere. It'd gotten really good at following me and offering me protection. When I was afraid, it was usually right there. Not now. Not in this place. DD was gone. I couldn't tug on the line between us, and I didn't feel it at all, which of course ratcheted up my fear—for me and what could've happened to DD.

When the sound of the evil laugh finally died down, I noticed a rustling. At first I thought it was the swaying grass, but it moved more purposefully in my direction. I watched as large blades of grass swayed, as if moved aside by something low to the ground.

I was frozen with fear, not knowing what would come my way, when from between the wrought-iron railing a large rat darted toward me. I squealed in the normal oh-my-God-a-fucking-rat kind of way, hopping from foot to foot to avoid it. It knew where it was going, had a destination, and stopped short of my legs by about two feet.

Then, it reared back to sit on its hind legs, its forepaws in the air and its face turned toward me. A small human face. A man's face, clear as day and twice as ugly, on the damn rat's head and body. It opened its human mouth, and a deep wheeze came out, as if its vocal cords were rusty but would work. Mine had no such restraint, so I screamed for real this time, a scream of terror at the ugly impossibility of what was in front of me and what had to be behind the thing if it was living there.

I bolted awake still screaming, Gareth's arms around me, shaking me.

"Randy. Randy! You okay?" he asked until I nodded.

DD was shaking, agitated, at my side. I sent a comforting tap down our line, relieved to see it was okay.

"What happened?"

"A dream," I muttered, now unsure of what I saw and if it even mattered.

"You and I both know you don't have regular dreams. What happened?"

I was trying to clear my head so I could explain as best I could when my cell went off, blaring and vibrating on my bedside table. I jumped, shaken, and Gareth cursed, reaching over me to pick it up and show me the screen. It read "Merry," so I fumbled to answer.

"Hey," I croaked.

"What happened?" she yelled. "Are you okay?" She sounded barely coherent, getting her own bearings.

"Yeah. A bad dream. Nothing to worry about."

"Didn't feel like a bad dream to me."

"Well, I have very vivid dreams," I grumbled as I eyed Gareth, who looked me up and down.

I heard mumbles in the background, then Merry said, "Harley says you need to talk about it."

Pulling the phone back from my ear, I saw it was 3:00 a.m. Shaking my head, I returned to Merry and said, "Will do, ladies, but not now. I'm going to try to get some sleep."

"Want me to come over?"

"No need. Not alone," I said, thankful Gareth was there for many reasons.

"Okay, sis. Try to get good sleep, and we'll talk about this soon."

"Yeah, you too. And Merry... sorry about all this." I felt like shit, not only because of the dream but what it did to Merry.

"Don't apologize. It's what I signed on for." She paused, then said, "Love you."

"Love you too. Later."

I ended the call, and Gareth jumped right in with "Seems the joining between you and Merry is working well."

"Seems so," I said, flopping down onto my back and bringing my arm up to cover my eyes.

"Hey. Randy." When I moved my arm to peek up at him, Gareth continued. "It's okay. A good thing, even. The fact Merry can feel you when you need her, even in dreams, is good."

"Guess so, though I hate to need it."

"We all need help now and then," Gareth said, easing to lie down beside me.

"I feel like I'm the only one who needs help. Like everyone around me is constantly having to do things for me or because of me."

"You saved my life not very long ago, if I recall."

I didn't answer. He wasn't exactly wrong, and I was more than happy Gareth was living and breathing beside me.

Gareth scooped me into his arms, holding me tight to his side, and softly said, "Can you talk about your dream?"

I shivered as flashes of it ran across my mind. "Not now. Not yet. In the morning."

"Sure," he said softly, tightening his hug before letting me go so he could turn us on our sides, setting himself up as the big spoon. "Will you be able to go back to sleep?"

"Eventually. I hope."

Gareth didn't say anything else, simply held on tight as I tried to calm myself. He was a natural calming agent for me. I managed to drift back to sleep after I spent an hour tense, worried, and guilt ridden. I definitely wasn't looking forward to telling everyone about my weird-ass and very scary dream.

# SEVEN

MERRY KNOCKED AT MY door bright and early the next morning. Too bright and early given the events of last night, in my opinion at least, but she and Gareth did have nine-to-five jobs they needed to get to, and she wasn't about to let me off the hook without explanations. At least she and Harley were nice enough to bring me and Gareth coffee from downstairs before they dragged me out of bed.

Gareth looked bright and shiny, as did the others, who'd all been ready to go about their days before swooping in to question me. I scowled. I was made for darkness, or at least that was what I muttered to myself and DD as it hovered a little too heavy at my side, like it was not ready to be up and at 'em either. Merry did allow me a few sips of a sweet cinnamon latte before she began her interrogation.

"About your dream..." She left her sentence hanging in the air, waiting for me to voluntarily pick it up. All three were facing me from across my kitchen as I sat grumpy and half-awake on one of my barstools.

Gareth looked worried but solid, his arms crossed over his chest and his feet planted firmly. Merry was questioning, searching my face and eyes for answers about how I was, most likely. Harley looked curious and aloof, her usual stance, though I knew care and concern was hidden there.

I didn't make them wait. No point in it, as they'd all pester me until I spilled anyway. I relayed the dream in as much detail as I could. Looking back on it, I realized how brief it was, how little information I'd actually gotten from it, and I still couldn't tell if it was a regular old nightmare or a super-scary dream-walking episode. It felt real, like dream walking did, but I didn't feel as in control as I had the last time I dream walked, when I'd interacted with Ny for the first time in his lion form. I didn't leave these assessments out either. They got it all, in my grumpy-sleepy voice strengthening with talking and the warm rush of latte.

By the time I finished, I was, sadly, wide awake and slightly wired from the residual fear memory pushed through my body. DD was perked up too, hovering in a more agitated frequency at my side. My magic thrummed in response, but like Ny taught me, I took a moment to clamp it down, calm it, push it to the background so it didn't get me all amped for no reason. DD followed suit, calming, though it moved closer to my face, gently brushing against my hair as if to comfort me.

Speaking of Ny… "You need to talk to the Prince about this," Harley said.

I knew she was right but shrugged my shoulders. I'd avoided Ny for a few days now, but something had already told me I wouldn't be able to hold him off much longer. At the moment, I was more concerned with something else.

Reaching a hand out to Merry, who met me across the cool stone of my countertop, I asked, "Are you okay?"

"Yes," she said with a smile. "I can't lie. It was scary, but not scary personally. I felt your fear and worried for you."

"So, good but not good," I said while biting my lip in thought. I didn't want this for Merry.

"Hey. I signed on for this, remember? I knew the consequences, which honestly aren't real big. Plus, Harley's been helping me meditate and improve my mental focus since we did the joining, which worked well for me last night. As soon as I felt the emotion in my sleep, I could put it to the side and function without it overwhelming me." She gave Harley a quick smile, full of something happy and light in this heavy conversation, but turned back to me with a slight frown after a moment. "I can do this, you know," she said, her voice sterner than usual.

I was caught off guard by her words and the force behind them. "It's not about you—"

"Sure it is, even if you don't realize it," she said, cutting me off quickly. "You think you can handle all this. You have no problem believing Gareth and Harley can do whatever. But me? Some part of you must think I can't do it, be safe and strong in this magic stuff, or else you wouldn't constantly bring up all this guilt and worry."

"Not true. I'm your big sister, and I'll always worry about you," I said as Merry leaned into Harley, who looked her way with a small scowl on her face.

"Yeah, hon. Worry doesn't necessarily mean there's a lack of trust," Harley said in reply.

"Feels like it." Merry looked between the two of us. "I want you both to know, when you do this, it feels like you don't think I can handle it. As if I'm not strong enough or smart enough or something."

"Merry Berry." I whispered her old childhood nickname as my stomach tightened at the sadness I saw on her face. I let go of her hand and moved around my bar, skirting Gareth and Harley so I could pull my sister in my arms. "I don't want you to ever feel that way. I love you, I trust you, and I do believe you can do whatever you decide to set your strong mind and will to do."I pulled back to look her in the eye as I said, "I'm sorry, Merry. The big-sister worry is real, but I'll try my best to rein it in from here on out. I don't want you to feel this way, and I definitely don't want to be the cause of your hurt or make you doubt for a second how utterly awesome and kickass I think you are." Looking over Merry's shoulder, I noticed Harley looked deep in thought. Didn't know what was going on in her mind, but my guess was she was feeling what I was feeling.

Merry hugged me again and mumbled about having to get to work. Harley walked out the door with her, a step behind my sister, with her head down and hands in her pockets. I thought about the conversation they were likely to have soon, if not immediately. It would sound a lot like what just happened to me, probably, and I didn't envy Harley in the least. If it helped Merry, I was glad it would happen. Glad it did happen between her and me. I never wanted her to feel less than in any way. Merry was more than. Always.

When I leaned my head down on the cool counter, Gareth reached over and rubbed a strong hand along my shoulders. "That was rough, but good," he said.

"I know, but the rough part was real rough."

"Yeah," he replied, giving my shoulder a squeeze as I pulled up to stand straight. "Ready for more heavy conversation?" he asked.

"Not particularly, but hit me, big guy."

"Harley's right. You need to talk with Nyarlathotep about your dream walking. You need to train with him as much as possible to help hone all your powers."

"You dream walk too."

"Yes. I do. When I try very hard to do so by using lots of power and intention, which is different than what you've done. Also, I don't share any other power with him, or, more importantly, you."

I huffed, knowing we were somehow skirting around a different issue. "I know you and Harley are right. I'll contact him today and set up a meet to discuss this latest dream debacle. You should talk to him about your dream powers too."

When Gareth agreed, I pushed on. "There're reasons why I resist, you know. Part of it is the magic and a certain fear I have about what it could do to me." Gareth hugged me to his big chest, stroking my hair to give me comfort I didn't feel like I should get in the moment. "Part of it is also the feeling I have around him, Gareth. The charge he gives me. The attraction."

I shut my eyes as the up and down of his chest paused, as if he held his breath a beat. I'd told him I wanted casual, and I did. He'd even agreed to it. I'd never said casual meant either of us considering the possibility of other people, especially Outer Gods who called me pet names.

Gareth pulled back to look over my face before he said anything. "I'd be lying if I said it didn't make me slightly jealous, but it has a lot to do with the possibility the two of you may have more in common than you and I."

I opened my mouth to speak, but he cut me off.

"No, Randy. No need to confirm or deny, or attempt to reassure me. I know you feel something with me too. You admitted as much yourself." He leaned down, gave me a slow, heated kiss before he continued. "You can't help the way you feel, Randy, and there's no denying there is a very real connection between you and the Outer God. I can't stand in the way of something that seems tied so tightly to your magic, especially if it means you come more fully into your powers."

"What exactly are you saying?"

"I'm saying if you want to explore your attraction to him, you should do so. We never discussed exclusivity, and I won't demand it of you now. Not with him."

My heart slammed in my chest at what the implications could be. "Are you letting me go?"

His eyes turned firm, hard as moss-covered stone, and he shook his head. "No. Never. Not unless you want me to let you go. What I'm saying is it won't mess up what you and I have if you also explore something with him."

"Are you sure?" I'd never been in an open relationship. I wasn't against it in principle, but I'd never tried it in reality.

He smiled. "I'm sure of you and me, what I feel when we're together in any way. I'm sure whatever magic is woven between us is strong. So strong even an Outer God wouldn't break it. Maybe he'd even add to it."

I didn't reply but hugged him tight. He was right about the bond, a feeling that grew stronger every day. Ny was a lot, but I didn't have this feeling of calm with him. I had something else, something I'd been denying because of Gareth. He'd opened a door, which was scary and exciting at the same time. Both Gareth and Ny deserved to know what was up, so more conversations of this kind would have to happen. Very soon.

# EIGHT

As soon as I sent a text to Ny—literally all it said was "I have a question"—the phone rang in my hand. I'd been planning on following up on the vague and slightly dramatic open-ended text as soon as I sent it, but he gave me no time. I didn't want to answer the call, mostly because I didn't want to speak to Ny yet but also because who even likes to have phone conversations? Shoving both aside, I answered with a tight "Yeah."

"Sweetling. You need me?" he said, his voice dark and sweet and thick as buckwheat honey.

"Well, when you say it like that... no." He laughed in response, so I kept going. "I need to talk to you about dream walking. If you're willing."

"I told you I would help with your magics, love. I'm more than happy to discuss the dreamings with you, amongst other things."

"Cool cool cool. Um... today? Are you free?"

"Always free for you," he purred, reminding me of the big cat I first met, now hidden away in the shape of a person. The big-cat shape was also a form of hiding, more than likely. What even was an Outer God really shaped like? It was too unknowable to consider, and at the moment I had more important things to obsess over.

"Okay. Should we meet at dusk again? The same place?"

"Yes, at dusk. No, not at the same place. Let's have a drink together." He rattled off an address much farther up on High Street, one I vaguely suspected I knew because of his insistence on me exploring the inbetween or whatever it was he called it. I ended the call unsettled but wired, worried and excited both. A mass of slightly contradictory feelings, really. DD, always in tune, jumped nervously at my side. We both needed to chill. Taking the time to still my mind, my body, my emotions with focusing exercises à la Harley, I shook it off as best I could and went about the remainder of my workday. I had a mass of trail mix muffins to make for tomorrow morning, after all, and they wouldn't bake themselves—even if the buckwheat honey I planned to use made me think back to Ny, to my conversation with Gareth, and to other sweeter, darker things.

YEP. NY WANTED TO meet at a haunted bar—the haunted bar, or at least the one most brought up if anyone talked about places that were supposedly haunted in Columbus. Char Bar sat in an old building, like many bars around the downtown and Lower Short North areas. It wasn't in either but more in the land between, not quite in the Short North but not really downtown either.

I'd actually spent a good deal of time here, since it was close to my old job at the Greater Columbus Convention Center. Surprise, surprise: cooks and pastry chefs liked to go out and drink after long shifts. I'd spent many nights in the dim, red-walled interior and wasn't exactly shocked to see it looked the same. Old, heavily worn wooden floors, U-shaped wooden bar, neon beer signs. I peeked into the next room through the connecting door and saw more of the same—old service tables and chairs, a few tablecloths strewn about, very little light thrown from the wall sconces and the setting sun beyond the large windows at the front.

Ny hadn't arrived, so I dipped back to snag a beer and sat at a table in the second room, knowing full well this was where he wanted to be. Or, more like, the rickety, slightly beaten door off at the end of the room was where he wanted to go.

The basement at Char Bar was where all the action happened, according to those who claimed to have had experiences in the bar. I could believe it, especially now with what I knew of magic and shadows and other crawly things in the dark. The narrow staircase down was made from stone, not the usual brick. Same with the walls in the basement. Gray slat stones piled high and tight with patches of brickwork here and there. The bathrooms were down there, a few larger tables to hold spillover if the night got slammed, and an old piano some people swore played itself, even though it was all kinds of busted down. Since Ny was so keen on me exploring those inbetween places so much, I'd bet anything we were headed down to the basement.

I was lost in my thoughts when DD vibrated with an excited shimmy, and my magical thrum went haywire a second before a purr hit my ears. "Hello, sweetling," Ny said with a smile when I looked up into his golden face. His face was achingly handsome, which should make me nervous but didn't, even with those fathomless, endless night-sky eyes boring down into my own. If I was honest with myself, it was my own emotions and responses kicking my anxiety into overdrive, not him.

As usual, I deflected. "'Sup," I said with a smirk and took a swig of my beer before gesturing for him to have a seat. He folded himself into a rickety old chair that looked like it was from a Pizza Hut circa 1988, and leaned back with masculine, feline grace. He was all grace, actually, the bastard. Enough to make a woman jealous while it also sent zings of other, more carnal feelings through the body.

"You called?" he asked, taking a moment to straighten the zipper on his always-present leather jacket. He wore a shirt this time at least. It was black, expensive, buttery material itching for a touch. He didn't have on leather pants today, but faded skinny jeans molded to his form and fed down into thick black combat boots laced tight.

All this made me speak without thinking. "How'd you get all this stuff? The clothes, the phone? And where even are you staying?"

"Why? Want to offer me space in your home?" he asked with shining eyes and a bright smile.

I snorted in reply, and he answered my questions.

"No one can magic things into existence, but one can magic their way into things already existing."

"So you stole it all?"

"Stole, borrowed, cajoled. Whatever you like to say," he answered flippantly.

"Kinda criminal of you," I said pointedly.

"The way you humans now hoard things as if a pile of inanimate objects matters is the crime," he replied, and since I couldn't really argue the point, I stayed silent as I downed the rest of my beer. I needed another and rose to get it.

"Allow me," he said, starting to rise, and I shook my head as I placed my hand on his leather-clad shoulder to stop him. My fingers heated at the touch, my magic raced, and I stepped back, retreating from the feeling and the hungry look he gave in return.

"No. I got it. You want one too?"

He nodded and smiled, so I went to the bar. I'd nurse this next drink because I didn't need a buzz, but I was thankful for the calm that a quick beer gave me as my hand echoed with phantom feelings.

When I sat back down, I said, "Can we chat while we have our drinks, or do we need to go ghost hunting immediately?"

"I'm happy to talk with you any time, Randy."

Silence stretched for a solid minute before I began. "I dreamed last night."

"Dreamed or dream walked?" he asked, leaning forward, interest clear on his face.

"I don't exactly know. The only times I've dream walked involved you."

"A special memory for me, sweetling, but you have the power, so it will not be the only time. Come. Tell me about your dream."

I did. There was no reason not to tell him. After I described all I could remember, Ny sat back in the chair, lost in thought.

"Have you seen this house before?" he asked.

"No."

"The face on the rat-man. Had you ever seen his specific face before?"

"Not that I remember."

He hummed. "Interesting. You know, humans cannot make up faces in their minds. It's an odd quirk you have. You need to see a face somewhere before you can visualize it, in memory or dream. If you truly have never seen that face, it was new to you and therefore real. Meaning you did indeed dream walk last night."

If the rat-man was real—the idea caused a shudder to race down my spine—the house was real. The cackle was real. The menace I'd felt in such a place was real.

"Last time, I dream walked to you and the black church. Does this house have something to do with Starry Wisdom too?"

He shrugged. "Could be. Could be some other reason."

"Not helpful," I muttered.

"I cannot give you answers I do not have, sweetling. No matter how much I wish to please you."

"Okay. Dream walking in this uber-creepy way seals the deal. I need to learn more about my powers, what I can do and how I can control it. Including this dream-walking business. You and Gareth can help me."

"Your librarian dream walks also?" Ny asked, his brow quirked in question and a sly gleam in his starry eyes.

"Yes."

"Delightful."

"You'll help me, right?"

"I've already agreed to help you, Randy. I do not need to agree again. I will add, however, you need to know more about all your powers and limits. We cannot focus on dream walking and ignore what else you may be able to perform. It will not serve you well to do so."

I swallowed but agreed. I needed to dive headfirst into this magic mess, and Ny was the best way to do it. Training with him was like swimming with a shark. He was a hungry predator. What he hungered for may not be physically painful, but it could take a bite from me.

# NINE

"COME," HE SAID, AN imperious command echoing in his voice. It was natural to him, though, this Prince. He was accustomed to people doing as he bade, here amongst humans and in the Dreamlands. Wasn't like the average human wouldn't want to listen to a voice like his, strong and sure and dripping in promise. Hell, I twitched to comply, to bend to him. Maybe I would one day, but this was not the day.

"A please would be nice," I said back with hard snark in my words. I remained seated at the scarred table, staring into his endless gaze. He closed his eyes and rolled his shoulders, the leather jacket he wore bunching and twisting so his tight T-shirt teased from beneath. When he turned, spearing me with his look, the thrum and call of my magic made me quake inside. DD didn't help either. It practically panted, clear as day for him to see. The traitor.

He smirked my way. "Please, sweetling. Do follow me. There is work to do." He reached a hand down, open palmed, to help me from my seat. I took it, steeling myself for the zing of power I'd get from his flesh on mine, the loud singing of my magic seemingly in tune with him. I wondered when it would ease, this riot of feeling and senses I had whenever I was around him. Or, maybe more accurately, when I'd become used to the feelings so I could shove them away with less effort.

He led us, hand-in-hand, down the stairs, as I'd predicted. As I entered the stone-lined stairway behind him, my hand still in his, he turned his head back and the door behind us slammed shut, leaving us in the soft, artificial glow of the single light above the stairs. Ny's eyes flashed, greenish eyeshine in his normally dark look. The mark of a night creature, a predator, the black lion he was. Yet, like with the black lion, I wasn't physically afraid. Others might have been, and probably should be. I imagined Ny took no shit and doled it out ruthlessly when necessary. The thrum of magic inside me, the calm of DD beside me, told me I was in no real danger from this beast. There were other dangers for me, things I wasn't ready to admit or explore, but I would be physically safe with him. I had no doubt in this.

We hit the basement, and I shook off Ny's hand. I noticed his own flex and curl in my wake, and a small part of me felt smug and satisfied with the sign of my own physical effect on him when he wreaked havoc on my senses constantly. Ny stopped at the old, dingy piano, the one so many people said played on its own, and struck a note with a tarnished key.

"A shame, to let an instrument waste away," he said, looking over his shoulder at me after staring at the keys for long beats.

"You play?"

"I play many things. Music is a particular interest of mine."

"I'm sure you're a regular pied piper," I quipped.

He smiled, big and sharp. "I have been known to lead people with music, though they all needed to be led, for one reason or another."

"So says you," I retorted, taking a step back to lean casually against another old table shoved against the rocky wall. "That's the way it is, right? Winners tell the tales."

"As much as I wish you to believe I always win, it is not the case, Randy. And I do try to tell the truth... when I can."

"Don't really like the 'when I can' part."

He stepped close, inches from my body, the heat and magic of him scraping along all my senses. "I do not lie to you, sweetling," he cooed.

"Exactly what a liar would say."

He smirked. "Touché, lovely. I see I need to prove myself."

"Actions speak louder than words, you know."

"Let us act," he said as he brought a warm, steady hand to my upper right arm. "Can we venture into the shadow world together?"

I stiffened, hesitant, and he said, "Trust I will keep you safe."

I did. Maybe against logic and feeling, I always had, so I agreed before straightening to steel myself. I hadn't been back to the shadow world since I'd dropped Macy there, and that hadn't even worked in my favor. Not too much, anyway. She was still around somewhere causing who-knows-what kind of damage. Plus, the last time I slipped into the shadow world from a basement had been the now-infamous—in my mind at least—Night of the Tornado, which had made me bury my magic for years because of the trauma. For sure not fun times. Had to admit, if I was going traipsing about in a land of monsters, it was slightly comforting to know I had my own big, bad monster by my side.

We flipped, instantly, to the grayscale world of shadows. DD sparked to life, radiating happiness in this place where we used to play so much. I sent a mental pet down our line, and it bounced in my vision, dipping down to skim across my shoulder in a barely-there whisper to give me its own type of pet in return. I smiled, comforted by the new familiarity of DD in my everyday life. It was a small, quick smile because I was immediately on alert, my head swiveling to check for slimy, hideous things, my ears straining to hear them.

"Randy," Ny called, snagging my attention. I gasped when I looked at him. His skin, smooth and luscious in the everyday human world, cast a golden glow here. It

spilled from him, shimmering and occasionally spark-
ing in spots. I grabbed his hand, holding it up to my
face, watching the glow trail behind as if a part of him
was a fraction of a second slower than his physical
form.

"Beautiful," I said on a heavy breath. Because it was.
Maybe the most beautiful thing I'd ever seen in my life,
the color and shape and movement of this light spilling
from him. "What is it?"

"It's my magic," he said simply. "It's the same in the
human world, you just can't see it there. Much like you
couldn't see them before." He nodded toward DD.

"I already learned to see magic on people," I said, half
in question. It didn't make any sense to me. Not much
made sense to me, so I guess it wasn't exactly new.

"My magic is different. From another dimension.
Not visible in your realm, though visible here."

"Why?"

"I do not know, sweetling. It is as it is. Only those
from my own dimension can view my magic in your
own, and as nothing from my dimension gets into your
own without a lot of very nasty workings, it does not
happen."

I frowned, unhappy with his answer on a lot of levels,
but didn't press the issue. The sounds started and I
was far more concerned with the slithering, wet things
making their way toward us. "They're coming," I said,
swallowing hard.

"Not for long," he said, and he snapped his fingers to produce a black flame. It shifted between various shades of gray and black but looked and moved like a flame in every other sense. A disembodied lighter flame bouncing around in some old black-and-white movie. When he'd popped it into existence, the sounds stopped, then faded, as if whatever had been drawn to us was suddenly repelled by the tiny non-flame thing dancing around Ny's palm.

"This," he explained, "is Dark Flame. A handy spell for anyone traveling in the shadows. It dispels the things which like to linger in these spots."

There was a lot to unpack in those short sentences. "What do you mean 'these places'? There's more than one?"

"Every plane of existence, every dimension, has a shadow version of itself. This is the shadow realm for the human plane, an echo of your world which serves many different purposes. It can be a place of monsters, of rest, of transition from one dimension to another. It takes magic to enter a shadow realm and skill to traverse it, use it to its full advantage. Something you need to practice."

"I might be willing to give it a shot," I grumbled, "since you have handy-dandy monster repellent."

He licked his lips, and with his non-flame-filled hand, touched a finger to my chest. Where he touched, my magic pulsed and throbbed, shaking with power.

"Did you jump-start me like a car battery?" I asked, baffled and slightly annoyed.

He laughed, low and deep, the sound hitting something low and deep in me. "Of a sort. I simply gave your power a small boost so we can practice Dark Flame without fatigue."

I nodded and said, "Okay. So hit me with the spell."

"It's simple enough," he said, using his free hand again, this time to trace a sigil in the air. His glow, besides being beautiful, was also handy. Whatever he wrote hung in the air a moment, suspended in his magic. "Pull your magic forward and draw this sigil in the air. Think the words 'Dark Flame' while also focusing on what you want, and you should be able to conjure it."

"I can perform spells without thinking of sigils now."

"You can perform certain spells based on your affinity with—and use of—Deep Dark without sigils now. There is a difference. Even I must use sigils and incantations on occasion to make certain magic work in your plane. This sigil is simple in structure, but Dark Flame is complex in execution. We start with the motion of the sigil, then in time, thinking of the sigil may be enough."

I couldn't argue. Whatever worked, right? I centered myself, dug into the focus Harley had helped me find, and did what he instructed. Nothing.

No surprise there. Ny made a noise of reassurance and opened his mouth for more, but I raised a hand.

"No need. I know how this works. It takes time and patience. As long as you keep the flame hopping around so those monsters stay far away, I'm good to keep trying."

He stopped his mouth and dipped his head, a silent encouragement to continue.

Over and over, I traced the sigil in the air and focused my intention. Even whispered the words to myself for a little extra oomph. Several times I failed. Until I didn't. I felt a tingle in my right hand, still raised after swiping lines and curves in the air. I looked at it and something slowly materialized in my palm. It wasn't a small flame like Ny's. It had more form as it materialized, and I instinctively wrapped my hand around it as it came into being.

In a matter of seconds, a torch sat, firm and real though created out of thin air, in my hand. It wasn't big, barely bigger than my hand, but shaped so I had to grip the small handle in my palm as I propped it upright. It looked constructed of solid shadow, black metal that swirled and twisted together, leading to a small black disc at the top where an even tinier sliver of Dark Flame danced.

"Impressive," Ny said, his head cocked in study of the thing. "Manifesting a vessel for Dark Flame isn't necessary. Did you think of this on your own?"

"I guess. When we talked about it, when you said to think about the words and intention, this type of thing popped into my mind."

Ny smiled. "Nicely done, sweetling. You did one better than me."

I blushed at the praise but did not reply, mesmerized by the dancing black flame I created in its own little shadowy package.

Thinking on what could happen, I said, "Can I do this in other places? Like use this in the real world?"

"There are several ways in which Dark Flame could be beneficial on your usual plane," Ny said. "More study and practice would be good."

I groaned. More studying. Of course there was more studying. Always with the studying and reading old books. "Okay," I grumbled.

"Randy," he said, firm enough to get my attention fully back on him. "What you have done is impressive and interesting but ultimately necessary. What I explained earlier was not solely meant to answer your question. I know you avoid this realm because of what awaits you here. Now, you have the ability to repel them, so you can explore the shadow world, connect with your magic here. I suspect it will help you strengthen your magical abilities on your plane as well."

"Why?"

"Because, like the cemetery, it is an inbetween space, and you, like me, gravitate to those spaces. Possibly find your magic works better in such places. This inbetween, however, is all shadow and shifting, which makes it align even more so with your power."

"Which is why I've always been able to come here," I guessed out loud.

"Precisely."

"Ny," I said, swallowing my fear and going for what I needed. What I wanted more than anything. "I asked Harley this once, but she didn't know. You... you seem more like me somehow."

He waited patiently for the long seconds it took for me to get the actual question out.

"What am I?"

His eyes, black shining night skies even in this world, softened, and he moved his free hand to cup my cheek. "You are a wonder," he said with a mix of reverence and vehemence in his voice. "Beyond that, I cannot answer."

"But you knew me, or at least knew about me, before we met."

"The Book of Knowing revealed you to me, long ago. However, not everything about you was revealed. It never told me how or why you have the power you have, or what it might mean about who or what you are at your core."

He stepped even closer, his chest brushing my own. My breasts tightened slightly at the nearness of him, and my breath hitched. DD blinked out, giving us privacy I didn't ask for.

"It did, however, reveal the truly important parts. All I needed to know. Which is you are a fierce, powerful, thoughtful, caring human woman who I will come to feel a great deal for by the end."

"The end of what?" I asked, breathless.

He shrugged. "The end of whatever time there is between us. Which, for my mind, will never be enough."

Too much, too soon for me. My life was far too complicated to even consider all he said, all it implied. He couldn't give me the one answer I needed, which wasn't his fault. He could give me answers to questions I didn't want asked. Again, not his fault. It all jumbled and tumbled around in my gut, and I was frozen by everything.

Ny sensed it somehow and took a step back, giving me space. He cocked a dark brow and said, "I also remember what you'll taste like in the future," he purred. The cockiness and innuendo I could latch on to and stoke, free up the frozen mess of everything locking up my mind and body. I suspected he knew it too. Gave me what I needed in the moment. As he so often seemed to do.

"That doesn't even make sense, in language or physics," I snapped, shaking my hand out and watching the Dark Flame disappear back into nothingness. I crossed my arms at my chest, half hiding my breasts and half presenting a stony front. Though it was all a game, it seemed. A dance. One he played well, and helped me navigate, toward an end point he knew would come despite my fight and stubbornness.

He chuckled at my words and body language and cooed, "Soon, sweetling." A repeat of his first line to me weeks ago, a refrain I knew would come to pass, even as part of me still tried to fight it off. For my own emotional sanity.

# TEN

NY AND I ENDED our night at the bar with few words. He didn't seem to need words. His endless night eyes trained on me as if he could see all the way to the dark of me, and his smirk permanently plastered on his lips said enough. I remained determined to fight the pull he had over me. The excuse of Gareth was gone, so the fight was waning. I'd always been stubborn—the old Carter fighting spirit. Even as my magic and desire felt the pull, something in my mind hesitated.

Had to be honest with myself and acknowledge I wasn't one hundred percent certain if the hesitation stemmed from fear of him or fear of myself and what he could help me unlock. I was so new to my magic, despite living with it all my life. New to trying to discover and control it instead of hide it. I knew, somewhere in my shadows, hiding from Ny was pointless. He saw me, all of me, including my magic, and wasn't afraid. In my mind, that was a big old red flag, but maybe it actually wasn't. Who knew? My head was done in with all this worry and learning and magic and looming disaster.

Which meant I had no words to give Ny after our time together, unable to parse through all the feelings and magic and thoughts crowding my head. I left him at Char Bar with a chin lift as a good-bye and made my way home, to veg in front of the TV with leftovers for dinner and, eventually, crawl into bed to lie awake for far too long.

When I managed to fall asleep, I dreamed. Dream walked right back to the creepy-ass old house where I stood alone on the cracked sidewalk outside the twisted and warped wrought iron fence. The dark night masked the house, making it look almost like shadows. One glowing window made it more real, gave off enough light to highlight the neglect of the place. The ramshackle, tore-down, sadness of it. The house could've been beautiful, given a team of highly trained experts from one of those house-flipping shows I liked to watch late at night. As it stood, no beauty remained. The eerie essence and funky smell of rot and wrongness didn't help matters either.

My mind wandered in this weird direction as I stared, unable or unwilling to move, I wasn't quite sure. A sound ricocheted in the night and made my blood turn to ice in my veins. A baby's cry, shrill and needing, came from the freaking house.

My body unstuck and I didn't hesitate, running through the gate, stomping up the rickety steps, and flying over the few feet of porch to slam into the solid door. It gave, no lock or other type of resistance in sight. Suddenly I was in a dimly lit foyer, one that may have been grand at one time but was now an old mishmash of waiting area and entrance. I realized the house wasn't a single-family house at all. It was a set of old, cobbled-together rooms for rent.

There were plenty of places like this in Columbus. Great old houses—even not-so-great or old houses—cut up into small apartments or double-wide single rooms to take advantage of the housing needs of those tens of thousands of Ohio State students rolling in every year. They were probably why the apartment I lived in existed; it was likely used as a student apartment at one point in time.

This place existed too far outside the acceptable OSU bubble, if it even was in Columbus. Too far removed to be choice housing for the average OSU student. Maybe a cash-strapped graduate student, but still highly unlikely given the general vibe of full-on neglect and waste. Regardless, it appeared no one had lived here in a while, what with the dust caked on every surface, hovering in the air in a visible haze. Cobwebs laced every available surface. I even ran into one, not knowing it hung in the air right past the door. I sputtered and choked, trying to get the sticky fibers off me. I wasn't exactly scared of spiders. Didn't mean I wanted their threads or their crawly little bodies on me.

It all stopped when the cry went up again, piercing the air and my heart. There was no reason for a baby to be in this place. No good reason anyway. It sounded from above, so I took to the wide staircase, racing as fast as I could to get to the kid, take it far, far away from this dreadful house.

I made it to the landing between the first and second floor but stopped dead when I turned to climb higher. There, at the top of the staircase, stood an old woman. She was withered with age, deep and craggy wrinkles all over her face. Her hair was falling around her head in feathery bursts, so wispy and barely-there it didn't seem right to even think about it as hair. Age spots dotted her face, her head, her neck, and the sliver of chest I could see under the sack she wore. It was an old time-y night dress. Like, full Ebenezer Scrooge. Though it wasn't nice and crisp. Rather yellowed with time and wear, stained in spots with things I didn't want to consider.

Her head was cocked to the side and her eyes squinted so hard at me I couldn't actually see them through the small slit and surrounding wrinkles. Her lips, thin as paper and nearly as white, curled into a wicked grin, revealing a toothless mouth.

A hand, fingers long and thin and stretched over visible blue veins, reached up to her shoulder and stroked something sitting there. It was the damn rat-man, sitting on his haunches, his rat arms folded over his belly in a deliberate way, as if waiting patiently for something. His face scrunched up in a clear sneer directed right at me, his black eyes unwavering.

The woman curled her lips at me, stroked the thing's tiny, clawed foot gripping her dirty sack of a gown, then threw back her head with a cackle. It would be cliché if it weren't so creepy. If it didn't whipcrack through the now-silent house. If it didn't send a jolt of pure fear racing down my spine.

She lowered her head, her eyes wide so I finally saw their surprising clear blue depths, and raised a gnarled finger at me. To mark me or beckon me or eventually flip me off, I didn't know. Really, really didn't want to know, because my stomach was rioting over the overwhelming feeling of unrightness the pair in front of me gave off in waves, an indescribable sense of horror and wrong I couldn't fully understand and never wanted to feel again.

I was frozen, by the crone in front of me or my own fear. Didn't know. Didn't care. I needed out. I felt it then, the tug on a line, a different shrill sound: the ring of an old kitchen telephone. I closed my eyes, raced for it, reached for the lifeline Merry gave.

I thought I felt claws on me, preparing to suck me back or rip me to shreds, but I reached the telephone in my mind, slammed it to my ear, and heard Merry say, "WAKE UP!" in her own frightened scream. Then I sat upright in my bed, drenched in sweat and holding my hand to my ear as if I held a telephone there, heart racing and mind reeling. Tears streamed down my face. DD zipped around the room in full agitation mode. My own fear for the unknown and unseen baby raged, though I suspected it had been a plot of some sort. Fear for myself also banged, hard and loud. A drumbeat in my ear matched the marching tears covering my face.

MAYBE THERE HADN'T BEEN a baby trapped in the awful dream house. I couldn't know. Merry called after I woke and talked me through my tears with her kind, soft voice, which soothed aches in my life. When I could breathe through the tears and form words again, I told her I was fine. I'd be fine, at least, and she should go back to bed. She reluctantly hung up but said she'd be by in the morning.

She wasn't lying, and she brought Harley with her, who somehow managed to look equal parts annoyed and concerned as she leaned against the gleaming stainless-steel workstation in the kitchen of Warm Regards. One bonus: terrifying dream walks meant I started baking bright and early. After I jolted awake, freed from the clutches of some creepy-ass old lady and her rat-man thing, sleep definitely wasn't happening.

"A familiar," Harley said, after I paused in describing the rat-man from my dream in more detail this time around. "Sounds like a familiar, which makes the old woman in your dream a witch."

"Great. Now I have the Wicked Witch of Shitty Houses after me?" I thought it was funny. Neither Merry nor Harley laughed.

"Witches are serious, Randy. If a witch is now involved, it means we may have yet another player on the game to contend with."

"So evil cults, familiars, witches, and Outer Gods. What's next? Is the Tooth Fairy going to get in on the action?"

"We're screwed if fairies come into play," Harley said, her voice and look deadly serious.

"There actually are fairies?" I gasped. "What else?"

"There are a myriad of magical beings in this world, and others, Randy. You've seen a few. Let's deal with those first before we start digging into other, darker corners."

Merry, looked between us, wide-eyed and worrying her lip. "What I don't get," she said, "is the difference between a mage and a witch."

Harley folded her arms across her chest, the neatly folded-up sleeves of her dark-green button-up revealing dark, sigil-marked forearms flashing tight muscles. Merry stared as if mesmerized for a moment, and I chuckled to myself. My sister had it bad. To her credit, she took the conversation seriously enough to shake herself out of a sexy-lady-forearms haze to focus on Harley's words when she began to explain.

"Mages and witches are similar in many ways. Both have an affinity for magic. Both know and wield magic.

Mages, however, use sigils to contain and expend magic and perform spells. Witches take it a step further. They empty a part of themselves, offer it up in sacrifice to generate their own magic."

She looked dead at me and said, "Witches sell their souls, metaphorically speaking, to have your abilities."

"What the hell," Merry whispered.

I said nothing, floored yet again by the weird shit I learned about magic and myself.

"I take it they don't sign the devil's book or whatever?" I eventually asked, wanting more but not really knowing where to start.

"No," Harley said with a shake of her head. "What most people think they know about witches is garbage created to control women and people of color over the years. Regular human bullshit. But witches are real. They aren't bound to a certain gender or religious expression. They do perform very heavy magic to make themselves into something else, something not exactly human, so they can hold magic."

"What's it mean for me?"

"I don't follow," Harley said, squinting her eyes.

"Am I not exactly human, something else?"

Harley stood straight, shifting forward to grasp my shoulder in her firm grip. "We've been over this, Randy. We can't say what you are beyond what you show us. Your actions aren't witch-like. You are you, which is good. For now, sadly, you need to be okay with that. Unless you want to dig deeper with Nyarlathotep."

I didn't say anything else. I already knew I was oddly close in power to Ny, an Outer God. Now I knew I somehow functioned like a witch, a person who was something other than human. Although what they did to be like me made them evil as shit.

"Randy," Merry said, shoving herself close and placing an arm around my waist so I was cocooned by the two women. I felt her warmth, her light... her goodness and kindness seep in. Merry's own personal brand of magic was something I desperately needed. DD turned it into a quartet, hovering close to offer its own special kind of vibrating support.

"You're you, Randy," she said. "The same Randy who protects me and Mia, loves our parents, makes kickass cupcakes, and cares enough about the world to take down an evil cult."

"Attempt to take down an evil cult," I grumbled, still stinging from discovering it hadn't actually happened.

"Whatever," she huffed. "You're my awesome, badass, sweet big sister, who also happens to have a buttload of magic in her for some reason. The magic, what it is and how it works, doesn't make you any less you."

My eyes were wet again, from love and appreciation this time instead of fear and worry. "Thanks, sis," I whispered.

She gave me a tight squeeze, and she and Harley both stepped back. "No problem," she chirped, before taking a sip of her coffee.

Harley leveled me with an assessing stare. "If there's a witch targeting you in your dreams, you need more dream walking practice. More knowledge of all your power. You need—"

"Ny," I said flatly, filling in for her. "I need more practice with Ny. I know, but it comes with other complications."

Harley chuckled. "I'm sure it does. Maybe call Gareth in as well. He's an experienced human dream walker."

I perked up. Gareth would help, no question. He'd also be a buffer with Ny. All for the good. "I'll set something up," I said, right before the magic in me thumped a deep bass note as if plucked hard. My internal timer. "Now, though, I need to take out these cream puffs before they get too puffy."

"Oh, speaking of cream puffs," Merry said with a dash of happy excitement. "I might've found you a good assistant. Someone who used to be in our home is about to graduate pastry school and is looking for a job."

Her bit of good news made me happy too. By home, she meant her job—the LGBTQ youth homeless shelter. Having an assistant, one who could give a helping hand, would be awesome all around. "Set up a meet and I'm there," I assured her before turning to grab my cream puffs and waving them off to go about their day. I had a mass of whipped cream to make while they cooled, and a lot to think about as I made it.

# ELEVEN

NY AND GARETH BOTH agreed to a late-evening meeting. I needed to bake, and possibly nap in the afternoon. Maybe sleeping during the day more would help with the scary dream walking, but it was really a wild, desperate guess. I was flying by the seat of my pants. The books Gareth had given me before, the ones outlining dream walking, were no help against witches and rat-men-creature things. I'd checked when dawn was barely creeping up toward day, needing answers and something to occupy my mind to stave off sleep.

My eyes felt like drop cookies left too long in the oven—crusty, dried balls no one wanted. I rubbed them, another bad habit never drilled out of me in pastry school, and continued on with my work. I had a wedding cupcake order to get through. Couldn't really decorate effectively, but getting everything done when I could was a solid plan.

I was knee deep in lemon curd when Mia strolled through the door. She said nothing at first, stepping up to my large pot to look inside. A finger stuck out, as if she'd stick it in for a taste, and I smacked it away. "No!" I screamed. "That's a good way to contaminate a whole lot of food and make me tank a health inspection if anyone saw it."

She looked sheepish and mumbled, "Sorry," as I dipped a tasting spoon into the mix and held it out to her.

"Take pics," I ordered, still a bit huffy at her attempts to stick her grubby little fingers in my food when she so knew better.

Still not really speaking, she went over and artfully laid the spoon with some fresh ingredients and a clean kitchen towel. The loud fake shutter-snap of her phone sounded before she scooped up the curd and stuck the entire spoonful in her mouth.

Mia pulled it out with a pop, a small smile on her face, and said, "Really am sorry, Randy. Wasn't thinking."

"Obviously," I said, in my best Rickman-as-Snape impersonation, a joke we batted back and forth often.

She laughed and pulled up, giving me a sideways squeeze. "Merry called me."

"Should I say 'obviously' again, or is it already covered?"

"Seriously, Randy. This dream walking stuff is getting scary."

"Don't have to tell me," I muttered.

She squeezed again before taking a step back and hitching a hip on my worktable. I turned and did the same, bracing for whatever she was about to say.

"I worry about you," she said.

"Duh. I worry about you too. It's what we Carters seem to do best, constantly worry about each other."

"Wouldn't have it any other way."

"It's annoying," I grumbled, "but you're not lying." I reached a hand out to pat hers on my table. "Are you here to tell me what I already know, or do you have something else?"

"Something else. Merry's call gave me info, but I was already planning to come this way." She scanned the room as if to make sure we were truly alone and said, "I've found more pieces of the book."

She didn't say the name out loud—the Necronomicon. Maybe as a paranoid tic or an actual precaution, I didn't know, but I followed her lead. "Anything interesting in the book so far?"

Mia shook her head. "Don't know. Can't read it."

"Can't read it how? Like don't know the language or can't physically read the writing?" With old-ass books, it could be either.

"Language. At least large chunks of it. There's English, like Shakespeare-level English, because of John Dee and all that. Those bits are easy enough to read. Other stuff is in a language I've never seen."

"You're not exactly a language expert, Mia," I said. "Let Gareth or Harley check it out. They're far more likely to at least know what it is. Harley for sure. She told me she had degrees in linguistics or something."

"True, and I will. A little later. I want more to give her. Hopefully the whole book."

"Where you at now with it?"

"I've managed to get about two-thirds of it, I think. More than anyone I've seen so far. The other one-third..."

Mia trailing off, not wanting to complete her point, didn't signal good things. She pushed boundaries, explored dangerous stuff in darker corners of the internet. I didn't like it, but it's what she did—who she was, as much as who I was being tied up in dangerous magic. I could fuss and worry and reel her back if she went too damn far, but I couldn't stop her from being who she was. Didn't want to, though it fueled the Carter worry a whole lot.

"That deep?" I asked.

"Deepest, darkest deep. Like beyond, beyond dark deep," she whispered. "Like I might not be able to get it, or might not want to see what it takes to get it."

"Then don't," I declared. "The book may be awesome and powerful or whatever, but it's not worth you losing sleep over. Believe me. Sleep is precious."

Mia plastered on a smile as fake as Barbie's and said, "I'll crack it, no worries. Always do. Then we'll have this fancy book and know all the answers."

Made me think of Ny, the talk of his missing book, and what it might hold. "Do you think this book you're piecing together will actually help so much it's worth whatever it is you're doing?"

"I think it's a key. A very powerful one that might unlock a whole lot of answers."

"You know all this isn't your responsibility, right? Just because you think you can do it, doesn't mean you have to."

Mia nodded but said nothing, the universal sign she did not agree with my statement at all but wasn't willing to argue the point. Fair enough. I was tired and unwilling to argue anyway.

I changed topics, told her about the possible new baking assistant. She told me about a funny video online, then showed me so we could laugh over it together. It was funny, and our laughs were genuine. In the background of our voices, however, below the laughter, the dark and worry still lingered. DD hovered a little closer, stock-still and somehow looking more vigilant than normal.

I MANAGED AN HOUR-LONG nap late in the afternoon, after Mia had left and I'd packed the lemon curd away for filling cupcakes later. I stayed on the couch, blinds wide and TV on, as I slept. Anything I thought might keep me from dream walking was good. Ny and Gareth might have more answers, more concrete help, so I didn't get sucked back to the creepy old witch house anytime soon.

The meet was set for seven in Warm Regards, in the café section. It was unlike our usual spontaneous meetings in the kitchen after one disaster or another happened. Being later in the evening meant we could have some quiet comfort in a space I enjoyed but still felt a little less personal than my apartment. Ny hadn't been inside my home yet, and I didn't know when or if I wanted him there.

Gareth arrived first, punctual as ever. I let him in the front door at his soft knock on the glass. "Hey, big guy," I said with a faint smile, leaning in to hug him tight when we cleared and closed the door. We stood close, a tad too long maybe, with me soaking in all the calming goodness from him.

"You okay, Randy?" he asked as he pulled back to look me in the eye.

"Peachy," I replied, sarcasm dripping.

His brow creased and he opened his mouth to say more, but Ny breezed through the door, energy crackling in the air at his arrival. DD, of course, jumped with excitement. So did my magic. All of it made me a little grumpier than it should have.

"How in the hell do you do that?" I snapped at him.

"You can do it too, sweetling. Don't act like you don't know." He gestured at DD, who perked up as always in his presence. I'd forgotten. Completely forgotten I'd practiced using DD to lock and unlock doors.

"But you're not using..." I trailed off. Didn't want to say DD or Deep Dark. I knew, logically, Deep Dark was everywhere, and I could call on it at any point. The little bit clinging to me, hovered in my sight and in my world, felt like something more personal and different. A piece of something larger, maybe, but MY piece. It was hard to articulate, so I didn't, even if I thought about it every so often when I felt something, or thought I felt something, from the little black ball in the corner of my vision.

"Deep Dark isn't necessary, lovely. Average shadows work as well, and they exist everywhere, including your flimsy locks."

Made sense, but still I scoffed and said, "Rude."

He stopped cold, a preternatural stillness taking his form as he stared into my eyes. It was eerie but not frightening. He shook it off as quickly as he'd thrown it on and dipped into a deep, stately bow. "My apologies, Randy. I will remember to knock in the future."

"Good," I called, stiff and haughty in an effort to once again stave off any signs of how he made me feel. How he made my magic sing.

I stopped short because I realized as soon as he entered it was like I'd forgotten all about Gareth. I turned back to him, an apology on my lips, and he gave me a rueful, knowing smile. "It's fine," he whispered, bending down to kiss me on the cheek. "I know."

He knew what, exactly? What Ny made me feel? How my magic called out for Ny? Or how bad I felt about it? Or how he also made me feel—different and more subtle but no less lovely or desired because of it?

I didn't have time for this mess, which is exactly why I'd wanted things with Gareth to be casual. Why he'd agreed to casual. Damn my messy-ass emotions and entanglements.

He grabbed my hand loosely, gave it a strong squeeze, and stepped away to face Ny. "Nyarlathotep," he said by way of greeting, throwing in a chin lift for good measure.

Ny stepped up, grabbed Gareth's shoulder, and squeezed. It wasn't harsh but affectionate, as was his sly smile. "Ny, Gareth. You may call me Ny."

I shook my head. On first meeting it'd been "boy" and "crawling chaos" and sharp stares and gruff rumblings. This was different and I didn't know why. Didn't have the time to delve into it either.

Earlier I'd arranged a small table, poured three tall glasses of berry iced tea—a summertime specialty in the café—and put out a few treats. I loved a good tea-service spread, even if it was technically too late to call it teatime. I waved the two men over, taking the single seat on one side of the table so I could face them both.

Ny took a deep drink of his tea, giving a sound of pleasure at the taste. It made my magic and my spine tingle. Gareth took a smaller sip but was no less appreciative. "Please," I said, possibly stalling a little as I waved at the plate of cookies between us. Ny took a sugar cookie with royal icing, one designed to look like a sunflower. It felt like an odd choice, the night choosing the sun, but I was reading too much into it. Gareth took a plain chocolate-chunk cookie, a favorite of his I'd included because I knew he liked them so much. He smiled at it, and a different, slower heat filled me at his knowing look.

Having the two of them here, together, and not at each other's throats made a whole different set of thoughts pop up in my mind. Thoughts I needed to shove away. Fantasies were nice, but we were here to talk about dreams.

# TWELVE

I CLEARED MY THROAT and got down to business. The details spilled out without much coaxing—the dream walk last night, the terror and menace of it, the inside of the creepy house, the witch and the rat-man. Gareth and Ny both interrupted with questions a few times, but for the most part, I told my dream story and they listened, attentive and thoughtful as I talked.

When I finished, Gareth sat back hard in his chair, a worried look on his face. "Harley was right. Sounds like a witch with her familiar."

"I thought familiars were regular old cats and toads and things."

"Can be," Gareth said, "though they usually hold some abnormality brought on by the processed used to turn them into familiars." He paused to take a drink of tea, possibly arrange his thoughts. "Witches are different to mages in the extent they will go to gain power. They want access to magic all the time, not access they need to siphon from other things. They still siphon too, especially when they've extended their internal power too much performing big magic."

"Harley told me all this," I said, not wanting to once again hear how horrible something people became to have what I came by naturally.

"Randy." Ny called for my attention. "Gareth is correct, and you should let him finish." It was a bold takedown, and I bristled. Who was he to tell me what to do? The look in his night-sky eyes told me who he was and made me back down. They looked as if they could see through me, to the heart of my fear and discomfort over this, and wanted to assure me that whatever Gareth had to say, it would ultimately be okay.

Gareth reached for me, maybe reading into Ny's look too, and said, "What others do or don't do means nothing to you, or who you are."

"What I am," I muttered back, "which is somewhere between an Outer God and an evil crone, apparently."

"You are something wholly new and different," Ny said. "Nothing like the ones who walk the path from mage or sorcerer to witch. Do not compare yourself. It is like comparing a lion to a leech."

Ny was the lion, not me, but I took his words in anyway, the small comfort they gave, and motioned for Gareth to continue.

With a squeeze of my hand, he started again. "Ny is correct; witches are far lesser. Literally so. The process to create a well of internal magic is harsh, requiring a ripping away of pieces of oneself. The internal self, consciousness, the soul. Whatever you want to call it. There is something in every human which makes them who they are and makes them human. Witches use spells to destroy chunks of themselves and set up a different, self-replicating spell to generate internal magic. However, it's still a spell, meaning it requires power and magic itself to execute. It sucks life force away—from people, animals, places—creating yet more hybrid creatures who are neither one thing or the other. Things forged with evil intent to generate and siphon power."

"What you're saying is to make sure the internal magical battery stays charged, they have to charge it by stealing life from and manipulating other things around them?"

"Yes," Gareth said. "You aren't like that, Randy. Please know this. Believe it. Your magic is intrinsic to you in the way the same internal consciousness or soul is intrinsic to others. It's part of you, and, I suspect, is animated solely by the same force which gives you life. Remember we discussed this before, the connection between your powers and your life, the first time we sat down to talk?"

"Witches have to kill to have magic, and I have to have magic to live," I said, an assertion more to myself than anything else.

"Nicely put, Randy," Ny said. "I told you before I was unsure what you are. Which is true, meaning you are no witch."

"Gotta admit, I'm slightly uncomfortable making witches evil. The whole women's oppression thing and all."

"In this case, it is poor semantics but only semantics," Gareth said. "The linguistic distinction gives us a name in English to work with, but it's an English thing, not an every-language thing. Even in English, amongst the occult, the term witch isn't exclusive to women. There can be witches of any gender."

Made sense, so I didn't press the issue more, which gave Ny the opportunity to jump in with a question. "Were you solid in these dreams?"

I leaned back in my chair with a thud. I hadn't even thought about the literal sensations in my crappy-old-house dreams and what it might mean. In the dreams with Ny, with the black church and his lion form, I hadn't been exactly. I looked it, when I saw my body in the weird old-school robe getup. I'd been injured from the pew, had the sliver of the magical wood come back with me and mess up my hand. However, I'd easily gone through the regular wood to find Ny's lion form, which meant the black otherworldly wood stuff was the sticking point, not me.

"Um, I think solid?" I hesitated, trying to remember. I had rushed up the porch, felt the rail under my hand, just as I felt the stair banister. I'd also opened the door with my hands. I think. Couldn't be too certain because it was messed-up, scary-ass dreams I was trying to remember.

"In your usual dream walking form, you should be less solid. Touch is less acute as a sensation, and harder to achieve. In dream walking, you must think about touching, feeling, in order to do it. It requires focus and practice. If you touched anything in the house, it gives us more information."

"What Ny says is right," Gareth added. The two men looked at each other with approval. They were far more friendly, and I was unsure what it meant.

"What does it tell you?" I asked.

"It tells me the house itself is something other, like the black church, or you were pulled into the dream instead of coming to it naturally."

"You didn't pull me to the black church?" I'd assumed he had, because it was his trapped power I'd gravitated toward when there in real life and in my dreams.

"No, sweetling. You were drawn there on your own. I exerted no will or power to make you appear there. Couldn't do such a thing because I was trapped."

I nodded. The sigil circle, the weird leather collar, and the overall magic of the church kept his power separate, and I'd had to free him before he could let any of it loose. He couldn't call to me beyond using his animal voice, something I do remember him doing. It was yet another mark of the way he called to me, of how my magic and my body gravitated to him, in and out of dreams.

Ny went on smoothly as if he hadn't made me come to quick realizations. "Did you feel power from the house itself?"

"No, not that I remember. Nothing like the feeling I got from the black church."

"Then you were forced there by someone, not the house itself. The witch, most likely. I doubt she wanted to have a friendly chat," he said with a hard look on his face.

"How is it even possible, slipping someone physically into a dream? This isn't *Nightmare on Elm Street*."

"Dreams are another reality, another dimension. Like any other, they can be warped and manipulated. Used to access a person or place if one has the power and knowledge to do so, and the place or person they wish to manipulate isn't protected."

Gareth's brow pinched and he picked up my hand—the hand that had sported his protection ward until recently. His look said it all, so I simply whispered, "Son of a bitch."

"I'll try to speed up the ward process, Randy," he whispered, setting my hand back down, "but it takes time."

"And until then, my dreams aren't safe."

"No," Ny said, his voice a harsh slash in the silence my sentence dropped. "However, we will make them safer much sooner than an adequate personal ward could be produced and set in place."

"How?"

"Training and practice." Ny paused and added softly, "Randy, you must work more with your powers, draw more on the well of magic inside you. There is so much to explore. So much that could protect and save you."

DD vibrated at my side, as if excited at the possibility. Or simply agreeing with the being it seemed to like so much. Either option pointed to Ny being right yet again, and me being behind because I was too stubborn for everyone's good.

"I know. I know. I just... it's hard. I spent most of my life suppressing my magic, and I'm still frightened of what it all means. What I might be or become."

"It is time to push past your fear and worry, Randy."

"He's right. You need to trust your power, explore it fully. It will help you, and everyone else around you."

Gareth had me there. Merry was deep in my head. Mia was off hunting some special book everyone and their mother seemed to want because of its power. Harley and Gareth had firmly placed themselves in my heart in different ways. Hell, I even felt a lot for Ny after this short period of time with him. I could do anything for these people, if they needed me to do it. They all put their necks out to help me. I couldn't do less.

"Okay. Okay. You're right. No more hesitancy from me. Promise. We'll get down to the nitty gritty."

A feline smile spread across Ny's lips. "Perfect," he purred. It was a literal purr. I could hear it clearly and feel it in my chest, where my magic thrum answered the apparent call with its own response. Gareth even felt it on some level as he shifted in his seat and leaned ever-so-slightly closer to Ny at his side.

"First things first, you must learn to defend yourself in dreams. Calling and commanding shadows works in dreams much like on this plane."

"I'll need help with this. I don't even know where to begin. Like, how do you even practice doing things in a dream walk? Am I going to be sleeping eighteen hours a day now or something?" Realistically it wasn't possible, but it sounded nice to me on some level. I'd slept so little lately, from fear and business and magical shenanigans. I needed to do all this magic business while keeping up with my baking business so I didn't lose my home. Not fun, but what could I do?

"You won't need to sleep all the time," Gareth said. "Meditation into other planes can give you practice."

"Like my solo vision quest thing?"

"Yes," Gareth answered.

"I will help you. Don't fret, sweetling," Ny answered.

"Me too."

"Will you help me together?"

Ny and Gareth looked at each other, and I suddenly thought of the afternoon meeting the night, facing off in some way. Something passed between them. What it was I couldn't say. It lasted a beat or two, then they stopped and both looked at me and nodded. We'd all work together on this dream-walking business to get my sitch sorted, and hopefully give everyone else a boost.

"Beyond the woo-woo magic of it all," I said, "we need to figure out real-world things too. If the house is real, we need to know where it is and what's hiding out in it. We also need to figure out if Starry Wisdom is behind it all. If so, great. At least we now have one enemy to worry about. If not, we're in some shit, because it means we need to battle two magical groups. BOGO isn't fun when it's foes."

All agreed, and agreed a discussion with Harley, Merry, and Mia was in order. If we were all in, then we needed to be in. Everyone had to be doing their part to get this mess sorted. Pronto.

Tired from this chat and the stress of life in general, I moved to officially end our meeting. Didn't want to stop hanging with the guys, so I went a different route. "Who's up for a drink?"

Both men grinned and stood, moving to my sides, surrounding me. Ready to follow. "Where to?" I asked, standing and stepping away, leading and knowing they didn't mind. "I'm in the mood for a good, fancy cocktail." Although I loved a dive bar, often preferred them, sometimes fancy worked too.

Gareth offered up a suggestion. "I know a good place in German Village."

"Then let's roll." I led them through the café, through the kitchen, and out into the night. Hopefully toward

a little fun and relaxation in the middle of all this
mayhem.

# THIRTEEN

I LED THE GUYS out, but once we stepped out into my lot, it became clear we needed better plans. Gareth had his motorcycle and Ny had nothing. In fact, I'd never seen him drive anything, so I made a mental note to ask how he got around. In the meantime, I didn't want to tool around town in my bakery van, and a rideshare to German Village at night would be astronomical. That left piling into the Mini Cooper like a clown car. I could take the backseat and let Gareth drive. No problem. In fact, I liked being a passenger princess sometimes.

Finding parking in the tiny cobblestone streets of German Village was hard as hell, but we were lucky and Gareth found a space about six blocks from the bar in a spot made pitch black by large trees and looming old stately houses. They weren't dilapidated like the house in my dreams, as these were the swanky, expensively renovated versions of Victorian houses in Columbus, but it still smacked of the same style enough to give me a tremor of residual fear.

Gareth led us toward a cute, squat brick building with a small patio enclosed in scrolled wrought iron. He peeled off to snag us a table outside, as the inside was tiny and looked cramped even from out here. He told me to grab him a Negroni, which he said was particularly good here. Ny walked close to my side all the way up to the bar, oozing his dark sex appeal so effortlessly it was a bit annoying. Everyone looked our way, something I wasn't exactly used to in places like this. He didn't care. His eyes, night sparkling with stars, were fixed on me.

"What do you want, Randy?" he whispered in my ear. The puff of air skittered across my nerves in the most delicious way, and I could practically feel the sexy-ass smirk on his lips.

I shrugged, acting nonchalant despite the fact I was actually chalant as hell. And damn if he didn't know it. He pulled away from my ear but casually slung an arm around the back of my shoulder as we both studied the specialty cocktail menu on the board behind the bartenders.

After a minute, a smiling woman with a lovely phoenix tattoo sleeve slid over and leaned in to get our drink orders. "A Negroni and an Aviation, please," I called. Ordering required some volume, even though it wasn't too loud, like some bars. I bent my head toward Ny, and he ordered a Sidecar. Seriously old-school, but then again all the cocktails in this place were old-school actually, which was pretty cool.

The woman nodded and went off to make our drinks. I didn't turn to talk to Ny. Not out of some avoidance thing. I was determined to stop my nonsense where he was concerned. I simply wanted to take in the scene. It wasn't my usual vibe, but I liked it. Tasty cocktails, mellow music, soft chatter here and outside. Swanky around the edges. All of it curated, cultivated, but in a well-done way. I could dig it.

The bartender was quick, and Ny was quicker in sliding her a few bills before I could dig my card out of my tiny keychain wallet.

"You don't need to buy my drinks," I said as Ny scooped up his and Gareth's glasses and left the smoky purple Aviation to me. I paused to take a sip before leaving the bar. I rarely drank gin, more of a vodka or whiskey girl, but I couldn't pass up the lavender. In sweets or drinks it was a floral note I loved, and this didn't disappoint.

"No, but I enjoy it."

"Why? I mean, isn't chivalry or whatever a human thing, and a fairly European thing?"

"Good manners serve well on any plane," he said. "You find something wrong with my behavior, sweet-ling?"

"No. Not really. Just seems odd for an Outer God, or any God for that matter, to be so polite."

"I come from a court. It is different from any court on earth, but it's a hierarchy like all courts on all planes.

There, politeness is both offense and defense, depending on how it is used."

"A fake tool then."

"Not necessarily fake, but civility, in any guise, can be a trap when it is forced or too rigid. I choose to be polite with you because I wish to be so, as a sign of respect. I may be cuttingly polite to others as a form of disrespect. I'm even polite and deferential when it is required for my own good, but such a thing is rare."

I opened my mouth to reply but something else caught my attention and took all my focus. "Well, shit," I cursed, true annoyance making my face heat. Not at Ny or what he said, because it was true, but at who I saw. Of course I couldn't get an easy night out with the hot dudes in my life. FML sideways, because seated at the table right beside Gareth at the outskirts of the patio was a group of several loud dude-bros in suits with a few women sprinkled throughout. Right in the center, holding court, was my ex-husband, David.

Ny asked what was wrong, because he didn't know my ex. Neither did Gareth, so I couldn't blame him for taking the one open table which happened to be right next to him. It was fine. I was fine... but actually, not really. It was weird to have an ex-husband. Because there was this dude who I'd been with for years, who knew so much about me—who I'd been, what my past was, how I'd felt about all of it, the wins and defeats over so many years of life—but looking at him now, I knew he was a stranger. It was truly surreal, to have a person out there who'd known so much about me, possibly more than anyone ever had before them, and now knew nothing.

Oh, well. There was nothing for it. I wanted my drink, dammit, and I wasn't going to let this dude who'd once ripped my heart straight out of my chest stop me from getting what I wanted now. I'd loved him once, fiercely, but the love was honestly gone. Hate didn't take its place now. It had for a long time, that negative emotion stemming from love had reigned because he'd still had a grip on me in some way. The love was well and truly gone, and mostly indifference took its place, the true opposite of love rather than hate. I was indifferent to him. Mostly. Seeing him annoyed me now because if he was who he'd always been, I knew he'd act like an ass when he saw me.

Proving yet again assholes rarely change, David's eyes widened then narrowed as he took me in, drink in hand and moving toward his table. He looked a step behind me, and I knew he saw Ny there. He then looked where we headed and narrowed his eyes at Gareth, who stood to take his drink from Ny and pull my seat out, ever the gentleman. Something in David darkened, by the look in his eyes, and he stood abruptly. Shit was about to go down, and David was about to instigate it.

He brushed off the lovely blonde woman at his right, who looked confused at his sudden movement. I felt for her, but not enough to intervene. I locked eyes with my ex, tipped my head in acknowledgment, and hoped it was enough. Ny and Gareth registered David and his looks my way, and they bristled at what his sharp-eyed look might mean.

It meant he wasn't letting an opportunity to be a shit go is what it meant. "Well hello, Miranda," he called. The name made my teeth grind, as did the smarmy tone of his voice. The men in his group perked up and turned to give me appraising, then dismissive looks. They likely knew who I was. The poor blonde connected to him somehow was still confused.

"David," I said in return, and Gareth stiffened. I honestly couldn't remember if I told Gareth what my ex's name was, but he knew it somehow. Ny, with his predator eyes, missed nothing in tone or look, so he was already on guard. He lounged, an arm slung over the back of his chair in a pose one might see as lazy... if a person had never seen a big cat hunting, lying still and relaxed right before springing into action.

On top of that, his magic unfurled, power coiling up and around. The hairs on my arm were raised. Gareth's sigil tattoos flared to life too, and I knew things could go south real quick if the situation wasn't defused in a less-magical-attack kind of way.

David, not tuned into magic and never one to think another person was equal to him, much less stronger, moved around his table to stand at ours. He ignored the guys completely, giving me an up-and-down. "Long time no see," he said, then smirked as if he found something too amusing for words. "You look the same."

"As do you. Cheers," I said, hoping to defuse the situation, but Gareth and Ny picked up on what he insinuated easily and did not like any of it.

Ny cocked his head like a cat and studied the suited-up man in front of us like he were an insect under a magnifying glass. "Who are you?" he asked in such a way every syllable dripped with disdain and dismissal in equal measure. Damn, he was good with the word battles too. Likely went back to the court thing we'd discussed.

"David Callum," he said, stuffing a hand in his pocket, signaling he wasn't offering them a handshake or any sign of goodwill or respect.

Ny shook his head and widened his eyes, a clear signal he still had no idea what his name implied or why he mattered in the grand scheme of things. A well-placed blow to a man with David's ego.

"Miranda's ex-husband," he said, all oily slick and saccharine sweet.

"Randy." Gareth gritted his teeth, meeting David's eyes with his own darkened green stare. He was apparently already done with this interaction.

"Nice to see you and all, David, but we're kind of in the middle of something. It looks like your friends are waiting too." I tried to give him an out, though the dismissal might have also rankled him some. Oh well.

"Oh, no, Randy. Let's chat. Catch up." He made a ridiculously exaggerated thinking-pose gesture, making the men at his table chuckle. "Thinking about it now, I'm pretty sure the last time we spoke, you were crying. Begging, more like it."

Snickers came from the other table. Ny hissed, literally hissed at my side, and his body seemed to vibrate with anger. DD wasn't any better. It was so rattled, it was almost jumping around my head, particularly frothing to be let loose on my ex.

I took a small sip of my drink as if none of what he said fazed me, because honestly it didn't. "Not the last time we spoke. That'd be at the divorce hearing, when I was more than happy to be rid of your ass."

"Don't twist it around, Randy. You didn't want the divorce, remember? All ready to work things out. I was the one who couldn't stay. Not with a woman who cared so little about herself she let her body stay like this."

He gestured up and down, adding to his not-so-veiled diss. I was too fat for him to love.

Ny purred. "Too much woman for a boy like you to handle?"

"Boy?" David sputtered.

Gareth stood then. David was no slouch. He was six foot and worked out regularly. He still looked small next to my big guy, all looming-biker scary right now. "You need to apologize, then leave," he said between gritted teeth.

"I don't need his apology. Would have to care what he thinks to want one," I said, feeling petty about him ruining my night.

Ny stood too, and with his stance, his power radiated outward, a physical thing even David seemed to feel because he visibly shivered. "Yes, boy. Time to leave."

A chair at the other table scraped back quickly. "You're acting like an ass, David. What you said was rude and totally fatphobic. I'm out of here." The blonde was stomping around to leave, and David grabbed her arm a bit too quickly, a bit too harshly. He was visibly digging his fingers into her skin. He'd never gotten physical with me, so this was a big surprise. How had he gotten worse?

The blonde let out a scared yelp. Gareth moved to grab David's wrist in a punishing grip, but in the instant David had touched her, Ny's power slithered out, a wet lurching thing, to freeze David in some way. He turned, wide-eyed, back at our table, and Gareth's hand dropped. David's eyes were shuttered, as if seeing something not really there, and he looked horrified. Utterly, truly, terribly horrified.

"Run," Ny said in an odd, echoing boom, and David did. He ran, flat out, like some indescribable horror were on his back, breathing down his neck. Maybe it was. There were invisible horrors all around. Maybe Ny sent one after him. He deserved it for the way he'd touched the blonde woman.

She stood, pale and shaking, so I got on my feet and moved toward her, totally ignoring about what could be after David.

"You okay?" I asked. No one from the other table stepped up to help her or David, so I bent to look into her face and get her full attention. "Hey, you're good. We got you."

"Thank you," she said, shaking herself out of her stupor. "That was... not great."

"Very not great. But trust me when I say you dodged a bullet there."

She forced a smile but didn't reply. I asked if she wanted a ride home or something, but she declined. She called a ride.

"I'll wait with you," Gareth said, ushering her with all his big-body, calming-voice, gentlemanly goodness out of the patio and toward the brightly lit corner of the busy cross street half a block up from the bar.

I plopped down and chugged my cocktail. No sipping after the mess of the last few minutes.

"What'd you do to him?" I asked once the purple liquid was all gone.

"Nothing he didn't deserve," Ny said, dodging the question.

"Fair enough." I slapped my hand on the table and turned a smile his way. "And for your recent performance, I'll let you buy me another drink."

He blinked at me, the angry fire bleeding from his eyes slowly but surely. He stood and bent over me, hands to the arms of my chair and inches from my face. "Whatever you desire, my sweet Randy."

I didn't reply as he kissed my cheek gently, almost reverently, and swiftly moved to get me another drink.

Gareth came back before Ny, looking anything but calm. He bent down, too, but took my mouth in a searing kiss. He pulled back after long minutes, and I asked, "You good, big guy?"

"Are you okay?" he countered.

"I'm all good," I said, letting the heat from his kiss warm my voice.

"Then I'm also good," he finally answered.

"Do I get some attention as well?" Ny said, back with the drinks.

"From me or Gareth?" I asked teasingly.

"Preferably you, because I need to taste you soon, but I'm certain both are delicious."

Gareth didn't fidget or laugh or shut him down. He simply sat back in his seat with his normal calm demeanor. I wasn't heated with annoyance any longer. That was for damn sure.

# Fourteen

WE STAYED AT THE bar. Because screw David. He'd ruined plenty of good times for me, and I wouldn't let him ruin this one. I had three cocktails. They were strong, much stronger than I realized until we moved to leave and standing felt wobbly for a moment.

"Woah there," Gareth said as he grabbed my elbow. He'd sipped his one Negroni all night, being the DD and all—though not my DD, who bounced happily around my head. Ny had another drink with me, but I'd been alone in my third. Lightweights. Smart, apparently, but still lightweights.

"I'm fine," I said, and I could feel the big smile pull my face up, making my eyes crinkle.

Ny laughed. "You are fine in every sense, Randy. Now, however, you may not be fully functional."

"I could run circles around you," I claimed, my defensiveness spiking. "Well, maybe not. But that's because you probably have some super-speed powers I don't know about and it's why you always poof in and out of nowhere."

"He's not the Flash, Randy," Gareth said, a hint of fond amusement clear in his voice.

"How do we know, huh? He could be."

Gareth had managed to move me from behind the table and steer me toward the break in the patio's fenced border. Ny slid his arm through my free one, pretty much trapping me between the two men as we moved onto the dark street. The light of the bar followed us, but not for long. The shadows of night closed in, but no worries. I had no reason to fear shadows.

Speaking of shadow, I turned my head quickly, trying to catch a glimpse of DD full on. I felt it there, at my side, silent but content. After a few attempts, which I knew likely made me look like an utter weirdo, I finally called out, "DD. Come." Like it was a dog or something.

It came, all right. Zipping to hover smack dab in the middle of my vision. I started talking to it out loud, something I rarely did. "You have fun tonight? I hope you did. You deserve some fun too. You work as hard as I do, poor thing."

Ny snickered at my side, and I glared at him. DD, for its part, beamed. If utter darkness could beam. It felt like beaming, anyway.

"Maybe two is your new cutoff," Gareth said, looking from me to the Deep Dark. His eyes were shuttered, a little wary, and a realization suddenly struck me. He was afraid of it.

"Don't be scared of DD," I said, leaning more against Gareth as I did. "It won't hurt you."

"Certainly not with Randy around," Ny said.

"It takes some getting used to is all," Gareth groused.

"Why?" I asked, abruptly stopping in the middle of a quiet cobblestone street. Ny kept my arm, standing tall and confident like some hero in a regency romance or something. Except for the leather, of course.

Gareth faced us both and said, "Deep Dark may perform your will, Randy. Same with Ny, I suppose. Doesn't mean you're the only ones who can control it. There've been plenty of mages hurt by it over the eons."

DD sagged in my vision, as if its feelings were hurt.

"Now look what you did," I called. "You went and made it all sad! Don't worry, DD. I'll always take care of you and defend you from grumpy big guys with an axe to grind for no apparent reason."

"I have reason and precedence. I don't hate it. Believe me. It saved my life in the black church. However, I also know the portion clinging to you is particular to you. Not all Deep Dark would or does behave in a similar way."

"Is that true?" I asked, looking over at Ny, who gave a shrug.

"I cannot tell you how any other Deep Dark would or could react to you, Randy. Gareth may not want to cuddle with our little friend there, but he is fine with it, I assure you."

I sniffed pointedly, letting the issue lie for now but wanting to still mark my general displeasure. DD was mine, and no one would talk shit about it in front of me. It appreciated the act and moved to brush itself against my shoulder before going back to its usual hovering spot.

The conversation, the walk, and the night and its humid vibe all worked to sober me some. I'd been buzzed, not drunk, but even that faded shortly. It left me with a soft, fuzzy, joyful feeling. We strolled along, quiet and slow. I took in the feel of these men, the sensation of being between them, and started to say a little too much out loud.

I stopped our ambling walk so we stood huddled together in the nearly silent street. It was a residential part of the Village, so not many cars crept by late at night. Before I knew it, I blurted, "You both make me feel."

The sentence didn't even really make sense. Maybe I didn't know how to make it make sense. It was difficult for me to express how both men gave me vastly different sensations I enjoyed equally. How I wanted them both and didn't want to choose between them.

I couldn't see Gareth's eyes through the darkness, but his body posture visibly softened. He reached a hand out to cup my face. Ny pulled me closer to his side, his body heat melding into my own. None of us spoke for minutes. We stood, feeling, which was enough.

"I want..." I said and licked my lips. My brain wasn't exactly ready to finish the sentence, but my body knew what needed to be said.

Ny suddenly hissed at my side, and at the same time, DD went berserk, zipping around in a tiny, tight circle.

"Someone with power is near," Ny said.

I focused and felt it then, tendrils of dark, old power wafting down the street. From the direction of my car.

"Do we meet it?" Gareth asked, the sigil on his arms flaring slightly in preparation.

"I fear we have no other choice," Ny said and moved to step in front of me—in front of Gareth—so he would lead the charge against whatever we were about to confront as we made slow, slightly stilted progress toward whatever waited.

What I saw when we were maybe half a short block from my car was Macy, smiling with fake brightness and coyly waving our way. A man stood with her, but he was hidden in shadows so dark I could only vaguely make out part of his shape.

Ny growled deep in his chest and stopped us all before he called, "Wilbur. I thought you were dead."

"Wilbur?" I asked. "What the hell kind of name is that?"

Ny answered coldly, "A very old one, at least by human standards. Although you aren't strictly human, are you?"

The figure finally stepped from the deeper shadows, making himself visible in the glowing light Macy posed under. Gareth gasped at my side, and for a split second, I thought he was gasping at the way the dude looked. Because he looked all kinds of jacked up, though it might not be nice to say. He was short, sickly pale with deep wrinkles in the sagging skin around his dark and beady eyes. A wiry white beard ate up most of his face. Sparse and patchy until it ended in a curlicue of a goatee. His lips were dull and thin, pressed together so tight to look almost non-existent under his gross facial hair. The hair on his head was also white, scraggly, coming down around his forehead and ears. Didn't cover those ears though, which were noticeably long and slightly pointed. All in all, he looked like a giant goat made into a man, or a man cursed to look like a goat. It was super weird and not a pretty picture. Something I wouldn't concern myself with if it weren't for the wafts of power and hate I felt oozing out of him.

"Nyarlathotep. I heard you spent your time on this plane carousing with these humans. I hoped it was not so, but alas." Every word he spoke dripped with disdain.

"Hi, sugar," Macy called, snagging my attention. "Miss me?"

"Not on your life, bitch," I said back with equally fake sweetness.

"Such language!" She gasped. "Where are your manners?"

"Not needed with the likes of you, believe me."

"Enough, woman," Wilbur bit out. Not at me, at Macy. She shut her mouth with a snap.

"You taking orders from Billy Gruff there?" I laughed.

"Silence from you as well, human."

"You say it like it's a bad thing, Goaty McGee."

Ny, still in front, touched my arm and shook his head slightly. I took the hint and finally looked back at Gareth, who I noticed had said nothing. Hadn't even moved. Maybe wasn't even breathing.

Shock, rage, and hatred warred on his face. Hatred won out. Pure hatred for the man in front of us. My heart lurched. Was this the man from Gareth's past? The one who'd killed his friends, turned him toward magic because of his evil act? I moved to him, placed a hand on his chest. Didn't care it meant my back was to all Wilbur's power.

"Gareth. Gareth," I whispered. He vibrated with pent-up anger and grief.

"It appears poor Gareth is once again useless, as he was all those years ago," Wilbur said with a sickly laugh. He confirmed my fears, and my anger condensed into a hot ball of lead in my chest.

"Shut your fucking face," I snapped. I'd had enough of whoever this guy was.

A wave of power barreled toward our trio at those words, and Ny stood tall, taking the blow. He absorbed it and staggered back a step on impact but otherwise looked unharmed, until I realized he was perfectly frozen in place.

"Ny. Ny!" I screamed at him, which seemed to wake Gareth out of his shock-induced trance. He moved to stand in front of me too, but I was having none of it.

I threw up DD as a bubble shield, which made a few cars and Macy tumble back at the force. Didn't do jack to the Wilbur fellow. It spilled around him, leaving him unharmed.

"Paltry power, girl. What I'd expect from a human, even if she exhibited more than the average person." His power shimmered, wavered, and he stepped right through DD. I felt it quake and punch against him, try to repel him, but it could do nothing against whatever it was this dude had.

Gareth lunged at him, going immediately on the offensive. The dude looked fragile in the way very old people often look, but he definitely was not. He shoved the massive bulk of a barreling Gareth to the side with no strain whatsoever, leaving him panting on the ground.

"I wished to meet you, Miranda. Measure you for myself. Much like these feeble creatures around you, I find you no match for me. More's the pity. A good fight may have been entertaining. Now I know you are simply a nuisance, one to be used then squashed at my will."

Gareth roared and pushed up from the ground to tackle Wilbur, but he was forced down by the man's power, pinned to the pavement. I shook Ny, trying to get him out of whatever freeze mode he was in, but it didn't work.

"Oh, he'll be incapacitated until I leave. I put something special in my assault because I knew what he'd do." Wilbur came close, too close. So close I could smell the rot and decay on him. It wasn't pleasant at all.

He studied Ny for a moment, tilting his head and rubbing his chin. "I will never understand Nyarlathotep. He has such power. Could rule this plane if he willed. Instead, he uses it to be among the humans. Find pleasure with them. Protect them." He spit out the last two words as if they dirtied his mouth.

I trembled. This dude was way out of my league and I knew it. Didn't mean I would give up. I pulled DD back because the bubble was pointless. My spear, however, might do some damage.

It materialized in my hand, and I crouched in the fight-ready stance Gareth had taught me. Wilbur laughed in my face, as if I were a big joke, until I lashed out quickly with the spear tip and sliced into his cheek.

He stood stone still, almost like Ny, and something black oozed from the small cut I'd given him.

"Not so funny now, huh?" I said, with false bravado.

"You'll wish you hadn't done that," Macy called from the sidelines with a laugh. Looked like she was back up and at it.

"I have plans for you, girl. Plans I cannot disrupt. Alas, you test my patience far too much. Such a blow cannot go unanswered." He moved lightening quick, too quick for me to track, and smashed my shadow spear to the ground before he pulled his right arm down then up in a backhand slap. The hit landed so hard, it sent me flying. Literally. Pain roared from my cheek out to the rest of my head in the long seconds I sailed through the air. My skull connected with the hard asphalt with a sickening thud, showers of pain flashed across my vision, and everything turned dark and cold.

# Fifteen

WHEN I CAME BACK to reality, I saw bright white everywhere. I might've thought I'd gone to the other side or whatever if it weren't for the constant, annoying beeping at my side.

My addled brain and blurry eyes cleared enough for me to recognize a hospital room. I was in the bed, surrounded by wires and tubes. Mia and Merry were slouched in chairs beside me, half asleep. Harley was staring out the grimy, dark window. Ny and Gareth sat, asses to the floor, hands over knees, and heads down in identical, masculine poses of worry. It would be a cute picture of care and love, from all of them, if it weren't for the beeping. Oh, and the pain wailing a sharp brass note in my head.

"Hey." My voice croaked, sounding scratchy to my own ears.

Everyone perked up, and voices rose at the same time. Harley strolled over to Mia and Merry, who jumped up and started chattering and fussing all at once. Gareth and Ny rose from the floor and hovered at the foot of my ginormous hospital bed.

"Wait," I called softly, and they all stopped. "My head is killing me. Can one person at a time talk, please?" I asked, looking pointedly at my sisters.

Mia nodded at Merry, who bent down and gave a sweet kiss to the edge of my forehead. It stung but the emotion warmed, so I didn't complain. "What happened?"

"Officially or in reality?" Mia muttered.

"Both, I guess."

Merry smoothed my hair down in soothing strokes. "Officially, you were involved in a hit-and-run. Suffered a massive concussion but no other damage. You've been out for a while. They were afraid—" She stopped, swallowed hard, and gathered herself, then continued. "The doctors thought you might be in a coma. Luckily, that's not the case."

"No, not the case," Mia said, "but the docs need to check you out ASAP. We have to make sure everything inside is okay."

I nodded and winced at the bob, pain radiating like lightening at the back of my head. "How long was I out?"

"About four hours," Gareth said, his voice thick and slow.

"Okay. Call in the doctors. Then you can tell me what really went down."

"Oh, um, you might want to also call Mom and Dad first. They were about to book flights when I talked to them ten minutes ago."

I sighed, in too much pain to scream at Merry but I did give her hard eyes. "Call them back. Now. No need for them to come."

"I'll try to talk them down," Mia said, pulling her phone from her pocket, "but no promises. And don't be all mad about it." Her eyes glistened. "We were scared shitless for you, sis."

I couldn't blame them. If either of them had been out cold for hours, I'd be out of my mind with worry, and I would've told Mom and Dad. Still didn't mean I wanted to deal with them now. Especially with some dude with masses of power and a wicked bitch slap prowling around Columbus. First to-do item: talk to the docs and make sure I'd stay functional. Then I'd deal with everything else.

AFTER RUNNING MORE TESTS, which included a lot of poking, prodding, and some time spent in the clicking whirl of an MRI machine—a first for me, and luckily I'm not claustrophobic—the doctors gave their verdict. I had a bruise on my brain from my skull hitting asphalt and rocketing my brain around like a ping pong ball. They didn't say it in those exact words of course, but it's what I imagined. On a positive note, no fractures or brain bleeding showed on any of the tests, and the bruised area wasn't massive. Yay for me.

Docs said I had to stay in the hospital until the next evening for monitoring. No less than twenty-four hours of beeping, antiseptic smell, and being woken or poked every two hours for check-ins. Plus, it made it easy for the cops to ask me endless questions about what had happened. I had a documented head injury, so I used it to my advantage. No, officers, I don't remember the car that hit me, or anything leading up to or after the fact.

The after-the-fact part was true. The leading up, not so much. I remembered Macy and Wilbur. I remembered it all, all the way up to the point when my head hit the road. I had lots of questions of my own to ask about it.

They let Merry and Mia stay in my room with me, which I strongly expected had some magic behind it from Harley. There was a bright, glowing ward on the hospital room door, courtesy of one of the mages or the Prince, so I knew we would be safe in this room at least. I still tried to convince my sisters to leave after the nurses wheeled me back into the room, mostly so they could rest in their own beds, but it was a no-go. They fussed and fretted and, to be honest, I was too hurt and tired to push back hard. Or, maybe, a good thing about all this shitty magic mess was I got better at accepting help and comfort when I needed it.

DD was deathly still at my side. So still, I worried for it. I reached for it down our invisible bond, offering comfort. It moved, slowly but surely, to my ear, caressing there. It felt sad and, I think, guilty. There was no reason for DD to feel guilty, and I whispered reassurances to it out loud. It had done awesome, as always.

"You're all good, DD. You did great. I promise. What happened is not on you. I'm fine."

It didn't get back to its perky self, but it felt a little less heavy after my whispered words. Merry and Mia didn't poke or question during all this. They studiously ignored my whispers to a thing they couldn't see but knew was a part of me.

However, they didn't manage to save me from a video chat with my parents, the traitors. Mom was in tears at the sight of me in a hospital bed.

"Oh, my Randy. My girl," she whispered as wetness streaked down her face, a tissue clutched close to her mouth.

My voice was still cracked and hoarse, so my reply of "I'm fine, Mom" managed to produce an audible sob from her.

Dad sat beside her, arms around her shoulders, stone-faced and angry. Very angry looking. Maybe more angry looking than I'd ever seen him. He peppered me with questions about the "accident" and what the cops had had to say. I feigned fuzzy memories once again, this time feeling worse about it because I was lying to my obviously distraught parents.

"Mia talked us out of getting last-minute tickets up there, but we're still coming up. Soon." Dad spoke with the brook-no-arguments tone all dads get at times.

"I'm really fine," I claimed, a little louder. I might've sounded a little shrill while also looking frantically at Merry and Mia for help. My parents did not need to be here, in the middle of all this mess. Potentially in the line of fire of the seriously evil Wilbur.

"Miranda Love Carter, you nearly died!" Mom wailed at my protesting.

I cringed, both in guilt and at the full name blast, which was a sure sign she meant business. Also, my middle name? Come on. Mine was by far the cheesiest, most cringe-worthy, although all of us Carter sisters had emotion middle names. It was a weird quirk our parents gave to us and one all three of us lamented to ourselves—and kept under wraps as best we could.

Merry tried to reason with them, her soft voice cutting through my panic. "Mom, Dad, we promise. She's perfectly fine. No need to spend money and time coming up now. How about we plan a trip down? Maybe the end of summer?"

"Nope. Not happening. We already got the tickets," Dad said with a gruff finality to his tone, and we all knew there was no stopping them now. "We'll be in at the end of the month."

I swallowed hard, my eyes wide with fear. The end of the month was a little less than three weeks away. How could we make sure they were safe here when they came in? How could we get everything under control by then, especially with that Wilbur dude roaming the streets?

"Mom, Dad. Randy needs to rest now. I'll call you back later with updates. She'll call you back when she gets settled at home."

We exchanged I-love-yous and take-cares, meaning all of it, but, for my part, I was frantic to get off the call. As soon as it ended, I was ranting to my sisters. "This is a disaster!"

They both nodded, grave looks in their eyes.

I needed help. Reinforcements. A plan of attack so all this magic-danger mess could be taken care of before my parents landed in Columbus. On that thought, another swiftly followed. Where was everyone else? I suspected I knew what happened but needed confirmation. Narrowing my eyes at my little sisters, I asked, "Is there a reason Harley, Gareth, and Ny aren't here anymore?"

Mia had the good sense to look sheepish. Merry was flippant, waving her arm in a blasé manner before she said, "We knew you needed the rest."

"First, not your call to make. Second, we need to plan, strategize. At least get some answers about what really happened and what it means. Third, Gareth and Ny likely feel like shit about all this."

The last part had Merry and Mia rolling their eyes, and I knew, instantly, whatever had gone down between the two men and my sisters wasn't good. "What did you do?" I asked between clenched teeth. It hurt my head, but the pain helped fuel my annoyance.

"They were there when all this happened, and neither of them were seriously injured," Mia said on a sniff.

"Because they'd been incapacitated by magic." I seethed. When both looked unyielding, I sighed. "Look. You weren't there. The Wilbur guy? Serious, serious bad news. Freeze-an-Outer-God-in-his-tracks bad news. Pin-Gareth-thrashing-to-the-ground bad news. I understand being protective, but they don't deserve any blame for what happened."

Merry deflated and muttered, "Harley said the same."

"She's a smart lady," I snipped back.

"We only yelled at them a little," Mia said.

"Likely made them feel shittier than they already did. You don't need to add to whatever guilt they probably already carry because I'm lying in this bed. Believe me."

"Okay, okay. You're right. We were scared," Mia said in a defensive tone.

"Being scared doesn't excuse acting like an asshole to people who are trying to help us."

Both Merry and Mia looked even more chastised after my big-sis lecture, so I didn't take it any further, except to say, "You both owe them an apology."

They agreed and that was that. People made mistakes. My sisters loved me fiercely. I knew it because I loved them in the same way. Sometimes fierce love made people do ugly things, for the good or the bad. Merry and Mia were good people and wouldn't aim to hurt other people's feelings unless they felt pushed to do it. Their big sister lying unconscious in a hospital bed was a push. I couldn't be too mad at them, especially when I thought about what I'd do if the situation were reversed in any way. I also knew, because they were good people, they wouldn't hesitate to apologize.

The issue settled, I told Merry, "Let Harley know we need to gather the troops. There're questions to answer and plans to plan."

# Sixteen

LOTS NEEDED TO HAPPEN, but maybe not necessarily in a bright, sometimes-crowded hospital room with zero privacy. Harley and Gareth were researching already, and Ny was out on some special assignment, so everyone on the outside was already working on it. We figured it was fine to meet at my place once the doctors let me go home after some final checks and tests.

The docs gave me their special once-over and came back confused. I wasn't exactly one hundred percent healed, but I was much further along than I really should have been. They found it odd. So did I, but I chalked it up to another weird-me quirk. I'd never gotten really sick before. Nothing beyond brief sniffles here and there. Never broken a bone or stayed in a hospital until this little stint. Never went to the doctor much at all. I'd figured it was a mix of luck and a healthy immune system or something. Now, I thought it might have something to do with the well of magic living in me. Not that I was complaining, especially when it meant my brain bruise looked a few weeks mended rather than a few hours. Yet another thing to go on my list of magic shit I may or may not ever understand about myself.

My sisters, undeterred by the doctors' all-good call, took all the notes and orders with many serious nods and lots of questions. They eventually gathered me and my paperwork up and carted me home, and I was genuinely thankful for it. I felt good propped up with a mass of pillows on my comfy couch. Merry and Mia still fussed over me, and I may have milked it a little. They could handle waiting on me hand and foot. Served them right for what they'd pulled with Gareth and Ny.

Mia had gone downstairs to swipe some cookies and pastries for our planning session. Merry fluffed pillows around me until I got annoyed and shooed her off. "I'm good, Merry," I whined with a wave of my hand.

"Fine, but I'm staying with you tonight."

"No you're not," I said with a pout.

"Oh yes, I am. If you don't let me, I'll call Mom and tell her you won't."

"Don't you dare," I hissed back, glaring daggers at my sister and forgetting all my thankfulness from earlier. The look slid off her like she was made of Teflon.

We were in Carter-sister-stare-down mode when Mia hurried through the door with a tray of tasty treats, followed closely behind by Harley, Gareth, and Ny. Mia stepped aside to set up food on the kitchen bar while the others continued into the living room area.

Oddly, the first thing I thought about was it was the first time Ny had entered my apartment. I loved my home, my space. It was very me. I'd wondered what it'd feel like to have Ny in it, changing the feel or whatever. His zap of power was there, for sure. He couldn't exactly leave it at the door. Surprisingly, it didn't overwhelm me or my space. His power mellowed, hitting the right frequency with my power. The feeling didn't calm, like it did around Gareth, but it did offer a sense of ease and protection. Rightness, even. DD thought so too because it greeted Ny with a happy shimmy in his face. He offered a small smile to DD and me, studied the space around, taking in me and my home.

Harley stopped at Merry's side, snaking an arm around her waist to hug her close and give her a gentle kiss to her temple. After that greeting, she turned to me and asked, "You good?"

"Peachy," I chirped with a harsh tone, still a little angry at Merry and her parental threats.

Gareth and Ny rounded the two women and stood a few feet away and faced me like men facing a firing squad. "Randy," Gareth said but halted. He shook his head. "Randy, I'm so sorry." His voice quaked at the end. I couldn't take it.

"Girls," I said, looking at Merry and Mia in turn. To their credit, they didn't hesitate. I knew they wouldn't.

The two stepped up together and Merry began. "We're the ones who need to apologize. We're sorry."

"Yeah," Mia grumbled. "We acted like assholes."

"We were worried for Randy," Merry said, with a quick look and contrite smile my way. "Made us a little..."

"Bitchy." Mia filled in the blank. "But don't you worry. Randy rightly tore into us, and we now see the error of our ways."

Merry stepped away from Mia to move closer to the men, reaching out to grab both their hands. "Honestly, you aren't to blame. The man who did this is the one who should take the blame."

"Truth," Mia said. "You're both great. Or, I mean, Gareth is great, I know. Ny, you seem cool and all, for an Outer God, but I don't know you like that to be able to make a judgment call."

I barked out a laugh. It hurt my head a little but felt good in my gut. "Okay, okay, you two. Awesome apologies." Looking over Gareth and Ny, who still stood tense in front of me, I asked, "Do you guys accept their apologies?"

"Absolutely," Gareth said.

"Yes," Ny said, offering a deep, low bow to my sisters.

Merry and Mia backed up, but I stepped in. Figuratively. I wasn't stepping anywhere at the moment, content as I was to lounge on my comfy couch. "Do you guys believe what they said? Because it's true, you know. What went down wasn't on you. Either of you."

"Agree to disagree," Gareth said in a quiet, deep rumble.

"Nope. Not going to happen. Both of you were held by really freaking strong magics."

"Be that as it may," Ny said, "we should have never been trapped in such a way, so what happened after the fact is a direct result of our mismanagement of the situation."

"I'm not playing this macho game, guys," I said, getting heated. "I'm no damsel in distress. I can hold my own. Do you believe I'm fully capable and can take care of myself in most situations?" Both nodded in agreement, and I went on. "If you believe that, then you have to let this go. We all do what we can when confronted with surprise magical foes or whatever. Don't blame yourselves after it goes down. It makes it seem like you're responsible for me, which makes it feel like you think I can't handle myself."

Gareth said, "I can see your perspective, but our issue is different. We care for you and don't want to see you hurt. Even if you can hold your own, maybe we don't want you to have to do it."

"Sweet, but in reality, tough luck, guys. With all this swirling, I'll be in shit again soon enough. You have to learn to deal with the possibility I might get hurt. I don't need to feel guilty because you all feel guilty. Make sense?"

Gareth nodded, but his shoulders remained tense. Ny looked from Gareth to me, then said, "Yes, but with the caveat we cannot always control our feelings, no matter what our logical minds say. We can, however, recognize them and try to work through them without letting those feelings control us."

"Good enough for me," I said. "Now, you two need to come give me a better greeting."

Ny moved first, sliding over to give me a sweet kiss on the cheek and whisper, "Glad to see you well, my sweetling."

Gareth took two giant steps to get to my other side, offering his own gentle kiss on the opposite cheek. He gave no words and flashed those moss-on-bark hazel eyes of his.

"Much better," I said, my voice sounding a little husky. "Now let's get down to business."

They situated the stools and chairs so they could sit quasi-comfortably in a circle around me and the couch. Mia handed out cookies and croissants and beverages. When everyone was settled in, I started with the most basic question. "What happened after I was knocked out last night?"

Gareth answered, "Wilbur and Macy left. They didn't say or do anything else. Wilbur wandered back to the shadow, Macy followed, and both were gone by the time Wilbur's magic dissipated enough for Ny and I to become unstuck."

"Okay. Next issue: Who the hell is that Wilbur guy?"

Ny spit out, "Wilbur Wheatley, the half-human son of my lovely brother, Yog-Sothoth."

"Wait a second. How did it happen? I thought none of the other Outer Gods could come down here. How'd one knock up some lady?" Mia asked, chiming in with the logical questions.

"A summoning ritual allowed him and a human woman to enter the same plane of existence. Not this plane, but one adjacent to it. Their union produced twin boys. Wilbur, who some of you have now met, and a nameless and invisible monster who was killed long ago. However, I don't know what may be true from those long-ago events. Wilbur Wheatley was supposedly dead also."

"He's sure walking around like a living dude," I grumbled. I noticed Gareth tense in his chair. His elbows were at his knees, his head down, his leg lightly bouncing. I called to him, and he looked up slightly, cutting eyes filled with hurt and fear and rage my way. "Is Wilbur..." I asked, not even wanting to finish the sentence.

"Yes," Gareth said, hate oozing out with the word. "Wilbur is the same man from my youth. The one who murdered my friends and nearly killed me. The one who turned me toward magic."

Merry and Mia gasped. Harley bit out a curse. Ny gave a heavy sigh. I looked at Gareth, hoping he saw how damn sorry I was about his past and how he'd been forced to revisit it because of Wilbur's appearance.

"What, exactly, is Wilbur Wheatley then?" Harley asked.

"He's not wholly human and not an Outer God. The second fact has driven him mad over the long years of his life. He has more power than any human, all derived from his father, but he does not have the full power of an Outer God. His entire life he's worked to ascend to such powers."

Looking around the circle of shocked faces, I asked, as gently and non-accusatory as I could, "If he's not as strong as an Outer God, then what happened with you last night?"

Ny leaned back in his chair, feline grace in human form, and said, "I do not possess my full power. We've spoken of this before. Without the Book of Knowing and the power it holds, I am not fully in my godhead. Hence, Wilbur was able to lock me in place last night."

"Like an Outer-God-on-Earth freeze ray," I muttered.

"Precisely. He tinged another spell with the older, stronger magic, hiding a spell in a spell so to speak, to take me by surprise so I could not deflect in time. It incapacitated me. Don't fret, sweetling. I know the flavor of his spell and his trick. He will not surprise me again." With the last part, his starry-night eyes darkened to something like midnight cloud cover, and I felt a shiver of fear and power rush through me. Everyone else must have too, what with all the communal fidgeting happening in the room. Hopefully no one else felt the thrill of lust spiking at his look and words.

I cleared my throat and asked Gareth, gently, "Are you okay dealing with all this?"

"More than okay. I've searched years for this man. I will not let him slip away again."

I nodded. No more needed to be said. "Whelp, at least we know the state of play for Starry Wisdom now."

"What do you mean?" Merry asked.

"If Macy was with Wilbur, it tells us a number of things."

"Like the power behind the cult," Harley said, picking up my train of thought.

"And what Macy's been doing since we took down the church. Doesn't tell us what the underlings are up to though."

"Not much." Mia chimed in with the unknown. "I've kept tabs on our unknowing mole. He survived, helped take down the shelter house. Talked vaguely about some others doing odd jobs related to cleanup and carpentry work. Otherwise, they seem to live in standby mode as of now. Whatever she's up to with Wilbur, Macy isn't dragging the human arm of the cult into things. Not yet at least."

"Good to know. Keep track of them, would ya?" I called to my sister, who gave me a "well duh" look in response.

"Doesn't this also tell us the Outer God responsible for your missing book, and the work of Starry Wisdom?" Gareth asked while looking Ny up and down.

"It's quite possible Yog-Sothoth tired of ruling over his cosmic holdings and bowing to me and my father in the Dreamlands." He paused, tilting his head and narrowing his eyes in thought. "Yet it doesn't feel like him. Yog is much more the smash-and-destroy type, not the plot-for-decades type. Either way, his baby boy is definitely responsible, so he will be held to account. Retrieving the book may require a return to the Dreamlands if Yog possesses it physically, but I hope not. Going there without my full power would be a fool's errand."

"Dealing with this Wilbur Wheatley will solve a whole hell of a lot of our problems," Harley said.

We all agreed, and she went on with the plan she had made while listening to all of us question and chatter. "The way I see it, we have two main objectives now. One, take out Wilbur and Macy, which helps Ny and destroys Starry Wisdom in one fell swoop. Two, figure out and overcome the witch house threat to Randy. We also now have a deadline, given the elder Carters will arrive from the Sunshine State in a matter of weeks." She smiled reassuringly at Merry and said, "We will do everything we can to make sure they have a pleasant, and safe, visit home."

"Yep, yep. It all sounds about right," I said, hoping to give encouragement.

Harley smirked at me and continued. "To achieve these two objectives, we need to do a number of things. All of us have to hit the books. Do more research into spells and the players involved. Everyone here can hit the books. Randy, you and Nyarlathotep must train more. The better grasp you have on your powers, the better off you'll be in any future fight. You especially need to work on dream-walking defenses and maneuvering. Gareth can also help you two. Finally, we may need the full Necronomicon more than ever. If we're dealing with a hybrid human with nearly the power of an Outer God, someone bent on achieving full power or bringing someone with full power to our plane, we need more magical firepower. The Necronomicon can help with all this."

Mia jumped in. "I'm about ninety percent there. Real close. The last ten percent is the kicker because it's the fragments most people rarely, if ever, see. I've developed a search algorithm I think will help, but it'll take lots of time and power to work." She laughed and said, "Computer power, not magical power, I mean."

"Do what you have to do. Let me know if you need any additional resources. I have a long reach," Harley said with a chin lift at Mia, who took the charge seriously, by the look on her own face.

"The plan is set. More specific research. More training. And more searching and compiling so we can hopefully have a few tricks up our sleeve when we see Wilbur again."

All agreed. The mood was heavy. I felt better despite it because I had a goal and a very firm deadline. I'd practice all day every day, go into any battle, and wade into creepy-ass dreams—whatever it was I had to do to get Wilbur, Macy, and the witch off my back so

Mom and Dad wouldn't find out what was really going on here with their daughters. Or run into any danger when they visited.

# SEVENTEEN

WHEN EVERYONE LEFT, MUCH later in the night
and after some much more pleasant conversation all
around, Merry helped me to bed and told me she and
Mia were crashing in the living room and would take
no arguments about it. She also told me she'd set up
an interview with my potential baking assistant bright
and early the next morning. I smacked a kiss on her
cheek. I was sadly behind in the baking business and
could use all the help I could get. Deb, my manager,
was a godsend, saving my financial ass and my sanity
any number of times—many of them over the past
few months with all this new magic business crashing
around me. Merry had found her, so I had high hopes
for this baking assistant.

I fell asleep as soon as my head hit the pillow and
wandered in a restful sleep. I became aware again when
the soothing darkness bled away, slowly revealing the
old house I'd come to dread. This time I materialized
on the rickety porch. Everything felt solid and real.
The old boards squeaked and groaned as I shifted my

weight from foot to foot. Just fabulous. I had got out of the hospital and was immediately sucked back into the scary dream walk again. Apparently, I was getting no rest from the wicked.

I was hurt, tired, worried, stressed, and angry. Like Vesuvius-lava level angry. It coursed in my veins and fed my magic. I brought the thrum to the forefront, focused on the power inside myself. Slowly, I ghosted, becoming like one of the wisps of phantoms from the cemetery, less physically grounded in the place. Couldn't tell how I'd pulled it off, but I'd taken over the power dynamic, for myself at least. I was dream walking here, dammit, and I'd do it my way. I stepped through the door without a problem and stood ready in the foyer, shadows gathering around my feet to give me a place to step.

Oh, the witch did not like that, not at all, given the rage-filled scream I heard from the floor above. Oh, well. Time to see what the hag was up to, and if I could figure things out about this mess while I was here and in control.

I sprinted toward the old stairs, then took then two at a time, shadows flying to keep up with where my feet landed and hit the grimy second-floor carpet. I found myself in a darkened hallway, warped but closed doors lining either side. Lots of rooms, lots of options. One farther down, the last room on the left, glowed with a faint light barely visible from the crack between the warped door and the dirty floor. Seemed like as good of a place as any to start.

I went in full steam, thinking swift surprise might be the best action. Once I plowed through the door, I skidded to a halt, unable to make sense of what was there. It was a regular bedroom, old and messy and caked with dust. It looked like a student's room, books and papers and other study-type things sitting stacked or shelved or haphazardly thrown around the space. Nothing shocking there. What was shocking were the equations on the walls.

A mass of them went from floor to ceiling. Some even spread onto the ceiling and the floor, which I then noticed was firm and solid under my feet. No shadows required with these things around. Numbers and abstract forms and symbols were well beyond my basic college algebra knowledge. Odd enough in itself, like something out of *A Beautiful Mind* or *Good Will Hunting*. What made it more odd, and made the hair on my body perk up in alarm, was the fact they glowed like sigils. They were equations creating or containing magic. Somehow.

Add a nasty-looking crack filled with the inkiest darkness on the opposite wall from the door, and the room was about as creepy as a math-filled room could get. Something serious and off had gone down here, for sure.

I moved to the wall to my left, squinting in the glowing haze to look more closely at the equations.

As if I could understand it. I discovered the equations gouged deep and dark into the dingy off-white surface. Whoever wrote them had born down on a pencil so hard, it had whittled through the plaster as it made its marks. The glow stood out and off, much like how Ny's magic glowed in afterthought when he moved in the shadow world. Except this was permanent, a wavy, hazy glowing layer of equation-sigils doing some type of magic, given the power wafting through the space.

A sharp cackle sounded in the room, and I spun around, searching the area. There was nothing, nothing but the crack, shivering and growing larger as I watched. The sound of the witch's hiss slithered out, along with darkness I didn't recognize. A thing cold and powerful. The darkest of shadows, so dark it had to be from another world. Whatever it was felt out of place, even as it called me forward, making me feel compelled and hesitant all at once. Big old warning sounds blared in my head, so no way was I messing with whatever it was, despite the call. It leeched out like a vine, like sticky tentacles, slithering out and over, coating the walls. With each glowing equation it hit, a sizzle and crackle of power sparked, like a bug zapper getting a juicy moth in its grip. Everything about it screamed "keep clear" in my mind, but the power it radiated, a power I somehow knew I could harness for at least some time, pulled at me. Asked me to use it. Nope. I'd read enough stories about the pull of dark and seemingly vast power, thank you very much. Not doing it.

The fascination broke when deathly white, wrinkled fingers appeared in the cracks, pushing outward, making room. A shoulder, bony and sharp, followed. I knew it was coming, but when the witch's head popped through, I still shuddered at the horrible look of it. The increased smell of rot and decay and wrongness permeated the room.

She turned her withered head, mangy hair clinging and clumping, to stare soulless eyes at me. Ice eyes. Blizzard eyes. Eyes I recognized a split second before she said, "Hello, sugar," in the saccharine-sweet voice I knew. Shit. That was Macy. Or Macy was her. The witch and Macy were somehow the same damn person.

I reeled back, the awful horror of the knowledge enough to steal my breath, make me weak in the knees. The woman I had nearly killed, the woman I wanted dead, the one who watched me bleed and wanted everyone I loved to suffer, was dragging me here for some purpose like she'd tried to drag me to the cross weeks ago. It was all her. Which also meant it was all Wilbur.

Fear snaked up my throat, constricting and trapping a scream there. Macy gave her signature giggle, hacked a cough as she lugged herself out of the crack to her waist, and cackled. The rat-man popped from the wall fully then and she hissed, "John. Restrain her."

John the rat-dude scurried over and, faintly, I heard an old phone ring in my head. It was Merry, trying to get me out. But I was frozen, watching in abject horror as Macy writhed to escape the wall in her old, decrepit form and a rat creature crawled up my leg to cling with its sharp tiny claws right in the center of my chest. He twitched his ugly man face at me and let out a high-pitched squeal, which somehow loosened my own scream. I let it rip through me, matching his squeal and Macy's cackle and the endless slither of the thing made from some form of shadow I didn't know.

The phone rang in my head, but the weight of John kept me pinned. It was some magic at play, I knew, but I couldn't do anything to stop it, much like Ny and Gareth couldn't last night in German Village. Macy was nearly free now. She slid around on the floor, her filthy, razor-sharp nails scrambling for a grip. Her body twisted to free herself from the knees down. The darkness bled further and further, closer and closer, still calling for me to reach out for it, save myself at some other cost. John scrambled up to my shoulder and sat squat and heavy, a small but dense lead weight I somehow couldn't escape.

I screamed, long and loud, and the two creatures in the room with me answered with their own ghastly sounds. I was about to reach for the new darkness to escape whatever Macy and the rat-man had in store for me, but right before I inched my toe toward a small tentacle writhing on the floor, I felt a pluck to the thrum of my magic. Something clicked in place inside me and power shot through my body. Enough power to topple John from my shoulder, to cause the dark nearly at my feet hesitate, to make Macy cover her eyes and wail out in pain and anger.

Freed for the moment, and the shadow-tentacle thing momentarily distracted, I sprinted in my mind to the phone, to Merry, to the tug down the line, which plopped me right back to my bed. Mia and Merry sat on each side of me, eyes wide and gripping my duvet, knuckles white. Ny was holding himself above me, as if pushing his body off of mine.

"What the fuck?" I gasped.

"I needed to share my power. Weight and touch helps," Ny said. "I apologize for doing it without your permission."

"Consider this to be blanket permission to do what you have to do to get me out of these messed-up dreams in the future." I wheezed, taking the time between words to breathe out steady and slow.

"You okay?" Mia asked.

"No. No, I'm not," I said. "But I will be. We all will be. Soon enough."

"Why?" Merry asked, confusion fighting the fear in her eyes.

"Because the bitch Macy is the witch in the house."

"What makes Macy being the witch any better?" Mia asked.

"At least now I know who she is, what she wants, and I'm going to make sure I kill her for real the next time I see her."

Merry and Mia seemed a little shaken, by the experience or my declaration of murder, I couldn't say. Ny looked angry and relieved all at once, a small wrinkle of concern etched into his normally perfect forehead. The single flaw made him more real to me, and my heart thudded in time with my magic, which I knew was partially his magic, at least in the moment.

"What are you doing here?" I blurted, fuzzy but slowly coming out of the haze of horror from my latest episode. "Not that I'm not ecstatic you're here, but how?"

He shrugged, pulling back and easing his posture. "I stayed close."

"Vague, but okay." I hesitated, then asked, "Stay closer, will you?"

A sexy smile creeped across his face as his power flared and my thrum answered. "As close as you wish, sweetling."

THERE I WAS AT seven in the morning, a horrible, creepy-ass-house dream barely behind me and staring at a fresh-faced young man of no more than nineteen as he looked around my squeaky-clean kitchen. I may have grumbled something about the cruelty of forcing darkness to meet the dawn, but he either didn't hear or ignored what he might have taken for goth ramblings. Instead, he stared at the setup, the equipment, and the supplies. After I woke up enough to actually pay attention to my surroundings, I stared at the way my shadows ran over him, as if they were excited to see him.

He wasn't a mage. There were no sigils on him. Maybe he had the potential to be? Or maybe my shadows were happy I was getting some help? Right then, mage or not, I needed the help, so I wasn't going to question him about it.

Ny slithered into the kitchen, tiny steaming espresso cup in hand, stopping both me and the new guy in our tracks. He leaned gracefully against a corner of my prep table and stared at the young man as he took a small sip of his hot beverage.

"What do you want?" I snapped at the Prince, gratitude for last night straight out the window.

He smirked and said, "You know what I want, sweetling." Want and lust and a twinge of sexy darkness leaked from him, seemingly without any effort. The potential baking assistant, Nate, stared. He looked dumbfounded and a bit shocked. Maybe also a little shy and unsure as red splotches creeped up his pale cheeks. For a moment, I thought, "Same, kid. Same."

Then I put on my snarkiest armor and said, "Out. Now, Ny."

He didn't listen at first and turned all his sexy power on poor Nate, spearing him with his deep-space gaze. He gave an obvious once-over to the now-frozen kid and let out a small huff of laughter. "He'll fit right in," he cooed, gave Nate a wink, and sauntered over to me. He bent to kiss my cheek, but I pulled back before he connected.

"Out," I said between clenched teeth.

"We'll chat about it later, lovely," he said before he stroked the side of my face with his own, as if he were scenting me like a cat. Or maybe like the lion he was somewhere inside.

Nate and I both watched, silent and still, as he languidly strolled out the room, steaming espresso pulled to his lips and his hips rolling oh-so-deliciously. Dammit.

A whistle sounded from Nate, deep and long. "Damn," he whispered. "Um, who is that? What's he do here?"

"Doesn't do anything but work my nerves," I replied.

Nate laughed. "So just here for eye candy?"

I turned and studied the young man. The shadows moved to caress him in spots. They didn't engulf him, like they did me, but they showed a level of interest in him they usually didn't show humans. Interesting, and Ny had thought so as well. Nate would fit in, and maybe learn more than the business end of baking, if he wanted to. First, I had to be sure he had the goods.

"I've read your resume. Saw you graduated from Columbus State, like me. You did some interning and part-time work. You're looking for full time now, right?"

"Yes, ma'am."

"No need for the ma'am business, Nate. It's Randy," I said with a smile as I pulled my hair up in a ponytail and ushered him around the kitchen. We chatted about his experiences, his favorite things to bake, what he wanted to learn, his five-year plan. When we circled back around, standing by the giant mixer, I asked gently, "You know my sister Merry from the foundation?"

I didn't name it, but only because I wanted to tread carefully. Didn't know if he had past trauma I might step into bringing it up, so I wanted to offer a simple out.

"Yeah. She was always super nice to me. I lived there two years."

His off-handed comment told me a lot about his background, whether he realized it or not. Two years without a home, not counting how many he might have lived on the streets before he found his way to the shelter. All because he wasn't hetero. It was enough to make me want to bash his parents' heads with my trusty rolling pin, even if I didn't really know this kid. No one should treat any kid like that, especially their own family.

To Nate, I simply nodded, gave him silence so he could continue if he wanted, but moved on quickly when he didn't fill it with more. He didn't owe me his life story, and I wouldn't press. "She's awesome, if I do say so myself. You'll see her around a bit. She likes to hang here."

"I also ate your stuff before. You know, when I was there," he said. "Dead ass, the best cupcakes I ever ate. One of the reasons I wanted to start baking and go to pastry school."

My heart lurched at his admission. I may have also gotten a little wet in the eyes. I brushed it all aside and gave him a wide smile with no tears. "Great. Means you also know what we do here. Right now, I need you to show me what you got. Make me something. Anything you want, complex or simple. I want to see how you and your flavors work."

He got down to business quickly, pulling ingredients, whipping through the kitchen at a high clip. He was quick, methodical, and clean. In less than forty-five minutes, he placed a small serving plate in front of me. Smack in the center of the gleaming white plate was a luscious-looking strawberry shortcake. The strawberries were ripe red with a hint of something dark. I took a whiff and smiled. The acid was sharp, sharp enough to point to a bit of balsamic vinegar. The shortcakes looked light and fluffy, a perfect little round puff with tiny specks of green throughout. I picked the plate up to look closer at the cake and Nate said, "It's lemon sage."

It was a new one for me. Sage in pie crust, sure, but sage in cake batter? I set it down and dug in, making sure I got a little of everything in my first big bite. As expected from watching him work and seeing the finished product, it was delicious. A simple dessert made into something surprising and tasty. The acid, the herbaceousness from the sage, the tartness of the lemon, and the sweetness of the strawberries with the fluffy finish of fresh whipped cream? Truly spectacular.

"You're hired," I said after swallowing the first bite. Nate let out a small, happy sound before I went on. "I'm really behind right now. When can you start?"

"Today."

Nate agreed to all the details of the job like pay and such, and we went about the admin business before we got down to baking business. I walked through recipes for a few hours, which helped me train Nate, see his skillset with Warm Regards bakes, and get a mass of stuff ready to fill the too-close-to-empty cupboards. Told him over the next few days I'd review all the standard recipes with him, then turn those over to him fully. I'd be concentrating on the specialty flavors, which changed weekly, and any special orders. With the way he was already performing, he'd get a shot at those too. In time.

"Thank you," he said as we prepared to leave after our long day.

"Thank you, Nate. You're a real lifesaver. I think you'll do well here too."

He grinned big and waved. "See you tomorrow."

"See ya," I called back before locking the back door behind him. With Nate, one huge worry was now off my plate. Still, the plate was piled high, and I needed to clear the messier parts of it as quickly as I could.

# EIGHTEEN

I PUSHED MYSELF UP my stairs, ready to take a bath and chill for at least thirty minutes after a long day. I found Ny at the top of the steps, waiting for me. Leaning all his golden-brown skinned, sexy goth-ish god hotness against the storage room door, to be precise.

"Ugh. Can I have a little, teeny, tiny break?" I whined as I topped the stairs.

"Afraid not, sweetling." Straightening, he cupped my chin and said, "However, I can give you a very thorough massage when we finish."

I grumbled wordlessly. Honestly, it sounded real nice, but I couldn't fully commit.

"You want to be able to pull yourself out of dreams, Randy?"

"Of course I do, Ny," I snapped back in answer. "You know I'm ready to train with you. I'm tired, okay? All this is new, and a lot, and I also have to still do things like run my business, which I've done all day today. So cut me some slack, okay? Me wanting a bubble bath doesn't mean I don't also want to kick some ass."

"Fair points," Ny said. "I'll leave you plenty of time for a bubble bath. I promise."

His lecherous smile was enough to make me laugh out loud. I hit him gently with my shoulder and said, "Come on then. Let's do the damn thing."

He opened the door beside my apartment as if it weren't locked and bowed slightly. "After you."

"Just because you can unlock something doesn't mean you always should, Ny. Sometimes it's plain annoying."

"Duly noted, Randy," he said with his blasé tone.

The storage room was bare, like always. Plain concrete floors, cinder block walls. The yoga mat I'd left behind was spread in the center of the small room. That's all there was. Ny made a *tsk* sound behind me. I felt a stir of magic in my gut, and I turned to see him holding a thick, folded woven rug in his hands. "No need for us to suffer. We're no monks," he said as he moved past me to spread the beautifully made mat on the floor and follow it down.

I sat to face him on the admittedly much comfier floor. "What's the plan?"

"The plan, dear Randy, is to practice certain methods of defense which may help you when dream walking."

"How can we practice when I'm not dreaming?"

"We reach a meditative plane. You've done so yourself before, of course."

"The same way I tapped into my power," I muttered aloud, more to myself than to NY, but he still replied.

"Some of your power. I believe there is still much to uncover inside yourself, but we don't have time to explore the issue at present. Defense and offense you can perform now is the most pressing concern."

"Fine. How do we get to this meditative plane or whatever together?"

"We touch as we meditate. Our magic is attuned and should guide us together without having to force the issue."

I wanted to ask more, but I didn't. It was the first time he'd outright hinted at the fact my magic and his magic thrummed in time. I'd sensed it for weeks. Even when he was in his lion form and part of himself, I'd sensed it. To know he had the same sensation around me made me feel a little better. Hinted at the fact he was as affected by me as I was by him.

He reached his hands out, palms up, and without questioning it, I placed my hands in his. The normal zap of contact hit and my magic thrummed tight and high inside me. I caught a glimpse of DD quaking in excitement and happiness at my side, before Ny said in a slow, commanding voice, "Close your eyes."

I did, and he continued in the same tone, guiding me down into a trance-like state, making me slip deeper and deeper into myself. Eventually he said, "Open your eyes, Randy." When I looked around, we were in my kitchen, prep tables polished to a high shine, and I saw the black-eyed version of me staring back at myself. Ny was firmly beside me but had no reflection.

"What's that all about?" I asked vaguely as I gestured toward the table.

Ny leaned in to whisper, "It's your shadow self. Nothing to worry about at the moment. She would never harm you."

"Why don't you have a shadow self?"

"Because my entire being is made of darkness and shadows, sweetling. No part of me, in any plane, can be separated from the dark without a great deal of powerful magic."

"Which is what happened with Starry Wisdom and your bro."

"Exactly," he said, a bite of anger making his word sharp.

"Okey-doke. We're here in my kitchen together. What now?"

"You wish to continue in your kitchen?"

"I control this?" I asked in return, not understanding.

"It is a place of comfort and peace for you, which is why you create it when you enter this plane. Your mind decides what we inhabit here. You can choose to make it whatever you wish."

I thought about it, but the kitchen felt good. It felt right. "This'll do."

He smiled at me, wide and open and a touch sharp at the edges. "Let us begin then."

First, he had me call DD to myself on this plane. I knew DD could travel between planes, of course. I'd first encountered it in the shadow world as a kid, saw it there when I went from my plane into the shadows. Bringing it here took some effort, but it came quicker than I thought it would. Within a few minutes, my little DD ball was proudly dancing at the side of my head.

"Now you know you can do it, you call your DD to you whenever you are dream walking. With it beside you, you can perform all your normal DD spells. Try some now, to get a feel for it in another plane."

I did, and it came easily with DD at my side. I did the bubble shield, the regular old shield. I zipped it around the space to cover lights and turn locks. When I called it into spear form, Ny, who'd been leaning against the table watching me perform, stood up straight, interest clear in the slant of his head.

"What is this?" he asked.

"It's a spear," I answered, a whole lot of "duh" sounding in my tone.

"I clearly see that, Randy. What I meant was why did you produce this particular effect? I saw it the evening Wilbur confronted us. I was frozen, not blind, but there were more pressing matters at the time. Now, I'd like to know more about how you first manifested the spear."

I shrugged. "Harley had me practice a whole lot of stuff, including creating a weapon from DD. This is what popped up when I first tried, and I kinda like it."

He circled me, studying the spear closely, before stopping in front of me and lifting an eyebrow. "Why do you think you produce such ancient artifacts?"

"I don't know what you mean."

"You wore a toga-like robe when I first saw you in dreams. You produced a torch when you created Dark Flame. Now you present a spear, which is a far more ancient style of weapon. Something rarely used in your day and age."

I couldn't answer. When he listed it out, I saw the pattern clearly, but I'd not noticed it before.

He stared deep into my eyes as if he might find an answer there but then seemed to shake off the curiosity. "More questions for another, less dangerous time, I suppose."

Agreed. It might well be something to look into. Later. When bitchy witches, rat-men, and half Outer Gods weren't on my ass.

"Now," he said, his voice sharp and accompanied by a quick clap of his hands, "we move on to new skills. Try shadow walking."

I waited, head tilted and eyebrows cocked in question, for him to explain.

He gave a broad smile and complied. "Simply put, shadow walking is moving from one shadow to another without crossing physical space."

I moved my eyebrows into a scrunch of confusion.

"Allow me to demonstrate." Ny stepped into a corner of the kitchen, where a long, deep shadow was created by the massive oven in the corner. He walked into it and slowly disappeared. I thought he'd camouflaged himself, like I'd done before with shadows, until he whistled from behind me. I spun to see him, arms spread out and a wide grin on his face, as he stepped out of a large shadow in the farther corner of the room.

"You're talking teleportation," I said in an awed whisper.

"More or less. It takes practice. First you must learn to blend into shadow."

"I already have that down."

"Very good. Then you must learn to become shadow. Once you are shadow, you can flit willingly from one shadow to another with a mere thought."

"You're sure I can do this? It isn't something reserved for Outer Gods?"

"Nothing is certain, lovely. Yet we still try."

I gave it a try. And failed miserably. For a solid hour.

My head hurt, my eyes were strained, and my skin felt tingly all over. I'd easily blended into the shadow, cloaked myself in shadow like I'd done before. Couldn't get past the cloaking stage for some reason. There was a hang-up about becoming shadow, I think.

"I can't do it," I said, frustration and embarrassment making an ugly, recriminating mix in my head.

"You will, Randy. You have the ability. I feel it at the edges of your power. You must trust your ability will guide you true."

"So it's trust I'm lacking."

"I believe so, yes. In many things."

Already annoyed and frustrated, I latched onto what he implied to dig myself out of more disappointment in my powers. "What's that supposed to mean, Ny?"

He moved closer, each small step a study in predatory grace. His eyes flashed with a night animal's refraction, like streaks of green shooting stars in a vast night. His head moved, ticked, in a manner which looked half human and half something else entirely. "You know what I mean, Randy," he growled, deep and low in his throat. "You do not trust your magics, and by extension, you do not trust me. Not fully. Not enough to give yourself to me."

"Why would I give myself to anyone? It's myself. The one thing wholly mine."

"Fine. I will quit euphemisms. You are sexually attracted to me but deny us pleasure in each other because you do not trust me or the way our magics react."

"Can you blame me, Ny?" I practically shouted, my breaths coming in angry heaves. "I don't know you. I barely know myself, with all this magic business. You're an Outer God who could hurt me in ways I couldn't imagine, body and mind."

His eyes cooled, his hand reaching for me, but I stepped away. He whispered, "I would never—"

"Don't promise never, Ny. There's a lot you can't predict, with or without your Book of Knowing, and never is a very long time for a god."

"The Book of Knowing knows you as well, Randy. Has revealed who you are to me, who we will be. To-gether. Yet you fight it."

"Maybe because I don't want a book telling me what to do," I yelled. "Maybe I want to be the one who makes the choice."

Ny looked sad when he whispered, "You always have the choice, Randy. Outer God or no, I am yours to command. I will wait an eternity for you if you ask it of me."

I stilled, taking in his words, knowing them to be true because of the thrum of my magic in my gut urging me toward him. DD, too, sat still, as if holding its breath, waiting for me to make the right choice.

"Good to know," I said. It was the truth. "Can we end our lesson for the day?"

Ny said nothing. He nodded and closed his eyes, and I followed suit. His voice sounded then, calling us back, back, back. Back into the cement room. Back into our real-world bodies. I opened my eyes and saw his face directly in front of me, thoughtful but not expectant. Not pushing. There, steady and waiting and understanding. As he always had been. As I guessed he always would be. It was a guess, I knew. Something that required trust on my part. Maybe even a little faith.

Well, faith was something I'd had little of my entire life, something I was apparently hungry for, because

I flung myself into it, letting my magic guide me as I leaned forward and kissed Ny for the first time.

# NINETEEN

I WENT IN SOFT, but the first touch of my lips to his sent a jolt straight to my gut, like a lightning strike to the top of the head. My magic flowed in giant waves, pulsing through my body.

Ny was stock-still until he surged, an answering wave of heat and lust, pulling me up and into his arms. Leaning me back, back, back as he deepened our kiss. He coaxed my mouth open with expert attention, and the first swipe of his tongue against mine was a flash of electricity pounding straight through my veins.

A purr sounded, deep and loud. I felt the vibrations radiating from his chest, and I clung to Ny's skin-tight T-shirt beneath his ever-present leather jacket. The purr and the slight scratchiness of his tongue hinted at his other form. His lion. Surprisingly, it didn't douse my desire. It cranked it up a notch.

Honestly, I was lost. Drowning in lust and magic. And I didn't care. I wanted more.

I pushed my mouth against his, meeting his urgency with my own. A moan welled up from deep inside me, traveling up my throat as if pulled forward by him. In a way it was. The simple kiss was enough to yank a moan of pleasure out of me for sure.

It seemed like hours and seconds, too long and not long enough, we had our mouths locked together. I was dripping with need, my breasts tight and wanting. When I started to writhe against him, hoping to get some friction to help alleviate the ache in my core, Ny pulled back. I may have let out a whining noise of frustration when his lips left mine, but I'd never admit it.

He chuckled. He didn't even look too affected by the kiss. Until I noticed his eyes. They were glowing darkness, literally. The whites of his eyes were completely gone, swallowed by the endless night which usually peeked through those irises. His gaze was space and time and true dark swirled and merging in a kaleidoscope of the deepest blacks and blues and purples. Like a nebula trapped in a bottle and surging to break free.

"Randy," he said, his voice containing an odd and ominous echo. He buried his head in my neck, his tongue slightly scratching as he gave me a long lick. "Are you certain, sweetling?"

I took the time to breathe, to think, and to feel. Feeling won out big time. "More than certain, Ny. I'm tired of fighting this. Fighting the pull of you. I want to feel all of it."

"Very well," he muttered into my neck before sliding a kiss from the crook along my cheek and to my ear, where he paused to give a sharp nip. "I will make you feel, Randy. The most delightful things."

He moved to my mouth and kissed me again, sucking my tongue into his mouth, where it vibrated with his purr. I pulled back and teased, nibbling his grinning lips in quick swipes before he caught the back of my head in his hand and slammed my mouth down on his. A growl sounded through his vibrating purr, the sound of warning from a predator. It made goose bumps prickle along my skin and my core to clench with need and want.

He pulled back to say, "We'll save teasing for another time, sweetling. Now, I promised you sensation."

Quick as a flash, he gripped my ass hard in his hands and hoisted me up. On instinct, I circled my legs around his hips, gasping at the scrape of his hard length against me, even though so much material got in our way. Pesky clothes did that sometimes.

Ny walked smoothly toward the door, and I got another reason to drool over his hip-rolling walk. It moved us both, punctuating each step with a smooth grind and withdraw that had me practically mewling in a few feet. By the time we were in my apartment, steps away from the bedroom, I was pleading incoherently.

"Hush, now," Ny said, a smile of purely male satisfaction on his face as he finally lowered me to the bed. Lucky for me, he didn't break our hip contact. Instead, he leaned in, ground down, and gave a luscious scrape of his hard, jean-clad length against me before licking up my neck again. He pulled back to look down on me, his eyes swirls of glowing deep space. If it was possible, they looked even more intense, more endless and fathomless than before. I paused, put a hand to his cheek, and stared deep.

"Your eyes..." I couldn't finish the sentence.

He closed them. "Apologies," he said, gritting his teeth. "I can normally contain them in my human form quite well. With you, it's much more difficult. I'll try to control—"

I stopped his mouth with a finger. "No. Don't. They're gorgeous," I whispered. I pushed up to place feather-light kisses on his closed lids. His purr kicked into overdrive, and I fell back to the bed. "And the sound?" I asked with a breathy laugh and wide smile.

Those eyes of his heated, and the circling darkness popped open to stare at me before he answered, "The purr is much like the eyes, lovely. Hard to control around you. However, there is an added benefit to this particular quirk."

Before I could blink, he shot down to his knees and was stripping my leggings and panties down to the floor in one smooth motion, leaving them to pool around my ankles. He offered no words, no teasing, no hesitation. As soon as he could shoulder between my naked legs, he bent and gave me a long, strong lick up my center, stopping to concentrate several quick swipes at the apex of my thighs. I keened, too full of sweet sensation to say anything coherent. He was right. The benefits became clear. The purr made his tongue vibrate. The scratchy texture heightened the feeling. Every lick and swipe shot fresh bolts of ecstasy through me. My back arched off the bed, I gulped down air, and in record time I finished on his tongue, letting out a scream as the climax ripped through my body, my limbs shaking and quivering in its wake.

He chuckled but didn't raise his head. "Again," he growled, and kept at the sweet torture of his tongue. He dipped down to swirl it inside me, deep enough to cause me to clutch around it before he focused again on my aching nub. He licked, stroked, purred, and growled until I found another release with his face between my legs.

I was panting, the tingling combination of orgasm and magic coursing through my veins, when he rose up from his knees. I watched, fascinated, as he slowly peeled off his clothes. He liked me watching, apparently, because he gave me a good show.

With a wicked grin, he peeled the leather jacket slowly down his shoulders, dropping his arms to let it fall to the floor when it reached his elbows. He winked, licked his lips, and closed those swirling midnight eyes as if savoring my taste again. His hands shot up and over, bunching his shirt in his fists at the back of his neck and ripping it over his head. I had a fleeting thought it was odd an Outer God moved like most human men when undressing, but my musings stopped along with my breath when he reached down to slowly slide his black leather belt out of its shining silver buckle. Next came the button, then the fly of his jeans piercing the silence as he slid it down without rush.

By all that was holy, he had no underwear on those tight-as-hell jeans, so when his fly spread open, it revealed golden-brown skin and a dark smattering of hair with a glimpse of his length. A small shove of his jeans, or a readjustment of his hardness, and I'd see all of him.

Ny snapped me out of my trance when he said, "Like what you see, lovely?" His tone was teasing but also tight with need.

I nodded and licked my lips. Ready to get going once again, I whipped my shirt over my head and finally kicked off my shoes and my crumpled leggings and panties. I reached for my breasts, squeezing them together and letting a moan slip through the sweet torture. "I need you, Ny," I said, bold and clear.

He wasted no time answering my call. In a flash, his jeans and boots were gone and he crawled over me, his heated tan skin feeling like licks of fire as it skimmed over my sensitive flesh. His hips slid into the cradle of my own, and I wrapped my legs around him again. I had to say, this naked version was so much better.

I looked up at him, his arms locked beside my shoulders so he held his upper body over mine, caging me in dark heat and comfort. He shuddered, his body wracked with some sensation or emotion I couldn't place, and his head dipped down to get a look at the length of me, at the place where our bodies met but didn't quite join. Not yet at least.

Looking back at me, he moved a hand to my face, brushed a stray black lock off my cheek, and gave me a serious look. "Sweetling. Randy. I need you as well. Possibly need you more than anything I've desired in and out of eternity."

"Then have me," I said, tilting my hips up to grind against him. "Take me."

He didn't wait any longer. Moving his free hand down, he slipped it between us to slide himself into me. He was large and long, and he fit snugly. No movement yet and he was already making my blood heat and pulse. My core fluttered around his unyielding length. He sighed, a sound of pure contentment, and remained still, his head bowed and face out of sight for a moment. Then he looked down at me, his own dark hair flopping in his eyes. Those eyes were bold and clear, easy to see in all their deep, dark mystery as he began to move.

The rhythm was natural, starting slow and gaining speed and force quickly. He muttered words in a language I didn't recognize under his breath, but I was too far gone to wonder about it. The rhythmic push and pull had me mewling like a cat myself, making high, incoherent sounds at the cascade of sensation crashing into my body. The driving, hard force of him hit all the best, deepest spots until I wanted to scream. There was also my magic, twirling and thrumming in

pace with his thrusts, spreading and unfurling as if
somehow growing with this contact. It was a daze of
feelings and sparks and movement, and I swear I heard
a song somewhere, even though I knew no music was
playing.

After a few minutes, Ny said, "I need more," before
he dropped down onto my body, giving me all his
weight. It felt hot and luscious to have him fully on me,
but it paled to what came next.

Ny snaked his arms under me, under my shoulders, curling them around so he could grip them from
underneath. When he had a solid hold, his thrusts
changed angle and pace. He went slower but harder.
Somehow deeper. So deep, I was seeing stars. It was
this side of pleasure. Not painful, but like nothing
I'd felt before. He hit something inside, sending stars
flying through my head at every pointed thrust.

I came with a feral scream so loud it made a burn
crawl up my throat. When my orgasm hit, my inner
muscles clenched around Ny and also took him over
the edge. He roared, a half-human, half-animal sound
so loud it shook the air. Darkness filled my eyes, but
I wasn't fainting. It was darkness coming to him, or
us maybe. Draping us in its embrace, shooting around
us in a swirl of sparkling black the same shape and
color as the fading edges of Ny's eyes. Eyes as open and
honest as him, staring into the heart of me.

# TWENTY

IT TOOK SEVERAL MINUTES for the darkness around us to dissipate, which worked for me. I needed time to catch my breath and calm my brain. That hadn't felt like simple sex. Not even simply good sex. Ny had played my body like an instrument, and magic had swelled during the crescendo. It was a lot to take in, but I had chosen to go down this road and had to face whatever music we made together or whatever repercussions came from it.

Ny was still inside me, though he'd leaned his body over so he was lying across my right shoulder, his face turned away from me. Didn't know if it was for him or for me, but there were things to do.

First: "We really should've talked about this, but I'm on birth control and clean."

Ny turned his head, his eyes his usual starry night, not his totally black, deep-space stare. He didn't move to pull out of me before he brushed sweaty hair from his face, then my own, and said, "It would take work and ritual for us to have a child together, and this body is immune to disease."

"Immune as in doesn't affect you, or immune as in you can't get or transmit them?"

His brows furrowed as he said, "Sweetling, I would never injure you or put you in danger willingly. You have nothing to fear from our pleasure."

I squirmed a little under him and he rose upward, finally pulling himself from me. I felt, then saw, he was still hard. "Didn't you come?" I asked.

He gave a dark, satisfied chuckle. "Oh, yes, sweetling, and it was glorious. It appears, however, my body is not done with you." He rolled off me, propping himself on an elbow. "Nothing to concern yourself with right now. As much as I'd like to fuck you all night long, there are other, more pressing matters to attend."

"Like talking about the black cloud of magic circling us a few minutes ago?"

He brushed my question off with a wave of his hand. "Merely an expression of the power we built together."

"What does that even mean?" I asked, the shimmery afterglow of my orgasms fading in my frustration at him acting like this was no big deal.

"It means we create a great deal of power when we have sex, which isn't surprising. Sex magic is not only incredibly pleasurable to produce but can be potent, depending on the partners involved."

I thought back to Gareth's sigils glowing when we were together, to the feel of my own magic whenever

I had sex. Made sense but was yet again another thing I didn't know anything about. Another thing someone told me after the fact like I should've already known.

"You could've said something," I grumbled, reaching for the throw blanket at the foot of my messily made bed. I tossed it over my body and rose.

Ny gripped my wrist, and I looked over my shoulder at him. He'd sat up in bed real quick.

"What?" I asked, pulling myself free.

"Don't run, Randy."

"Not running, Ny. I need to go to the bathroom. Clean myself up, use the bathroom so I don't get a UTI. You know, regular human woman things."

"You're annoyed with me," he whispered, dropping my hand and looking confused.

I barked out a laugh. "You think? Whatever gave it away, oh, powerful and all-knowing Prince of the Dreamlands?"

In a flash, he was no longer on the bed. He had me tight in his arms, staring down into my face with a steely look on his face. "Don't mock. Not after what occurred moments ago. Do you think what we experienced in your bed means so little?"

"I don't know what it means, Ny, because you didn't tell me. You didn't tell me anything about sex magic or whatever. How am I supposed to know if it was something special or if it was a regular weeknight romp for you?"

He leaned into me, shifting my weight to hold my body tight in one arm as he cradled my head in the palm of his other hand. He stroked the shell of my ear with his tongue before he whispered into it, into my very soul. "What we have is written in the very stars and burns dark enough to bring entire realms to their knees." He pulled back to look into my eyes, and emotion clouded his voice. "Do not mistake my contentment for disregard. I have had little in my long life to make me feel content, so those moments with you have been precious. Will remain precious. Will forever be precious if I'm lucky enough to experience them again in the future."

He righted me and I was speechless, so I nodded. After a beat, I said, "I just—" but he cut me off with a shake of his head.

"You are new to me. It is something I must remember. As well as the fact you don't have the knowledge of magic, the knowledge of us, yet. I wasn't mindful after a very pleasurable time spent inside you. We both mis-stepped, I think."

"Sounds about right," I grumbled before giving him a big squeeze with one arm while the other held my throw between us. Our naked bodies touching might ignite quick blaze of lust, and I didn't think I could handle more sex with Ny tonight. Better safe than sorry, even if it meant fewer orgasms at the end of the day.

"Let's get you clean and keep your luscious body in order." Before I could protest, he swept me up in his arms and carried me to the bathroom, my full weight nothing to his godliness or his general care of me. After I assured him I was fine on my own, I shut the bathroom door and blew out a breath. I'd feared what might happen if Ny and I hooked up, and my fears weren't exactly put to rest. I hoped my mind and my body were up to a scary challenge.

I MADE US A quick breakfast-for-dinner spread with eggs, sausage links, and french toast made with brioche I had lying around. We needed to chat, about a number of things, but I was starving. Sex could do that to a girl. Better to feed myself while we had necessary conversation.

Ny had impeccable table manners. We sat across from each other at the sleek, dark-wooden dining table squeezed between the kitchen bar and the living room. It was used when people were over for a meal, so it felt a little special when I sat down with someone to eat there. Ny looked at the plate I had set in front of him and grinned widely, though he waited for me to have a seat. He spread a napkin on his lap, held his fork and butterknife elegantly, and ate in small bites he smoothly cut. I dug in, not caring about manners at the moment. I did manage to not talk with my mouth full.

"You need to explain sex magic a little more," I said between bites.

Ny sipped the glass of water at his side before he answered. "It is energy exchange in its most basic form. When humans or any other beings on this plane have sex, they create excess energy. This energy can dissipate, hitting the air to be absorbed into other things eventually. It can be internalized to fuel one's own magic. Or, it can be cast in the moment by someone with intention, focus, and a particular spell."

"Is it powerful?"

"Maybe the most powerful natural form of producing magic amongst humans." He took a bite of syrup-drenched french toast, gave a soft moan, and licked his lips clean. My blood heated instantly in response. "It is certainly the most enjoyable," he said, his eyes locked with mine and heat adding weight to his night-sky gaze.

I cleared my throat and looked down to push some egg around my plate. "The different options are to let it float away, store it somehow, or use it right then."

"Yes. Tonight, we had no use for the magic, and neither one of us needs to reinforce our own magics by storing what we created. What you saw was the vast amount of magic we made swirling until it faded into something else."

"What else?"

He shrugged. "I can't tell you, Randy. I don't know. Maybe it bled into the air, the flooring, the walls, out into the night to be captured by some mage far away. But it went somewhere."

"Because energy doesn't disappear, it changes," I muttered. Funny how my physics class in high school kept popping up in my thirties.

"Precisely."

We ate in easy silence for a few minutes before I took us down another conversational path. "I spoke with Gareth about you," I said, slow but steady.

"I'm sure you did," he replied without showing any reaction.

"We've never really talked about Gareth."

"No, we have not. I don't see a need, but if it would make you feel better, I'm ready to listen," he said as he finished off his sausage.

"Well, see. We talked about you. And me. Us, together. He knows I feel something for you. You have to know I also feel something for him."

"Randy. Lovely." He put his utensils down neatly on his finished plate and reached for my hands. I gave them to him, ready to hear whatever he wanted to say. I'd given Gareth the chance to voice his feelings or concerns. Ny deserved the same. "Do you really think I do not know you enjoy having sex with Gareth?"

It was an odd question but made me want to see where he'd take this, so I shook my head. He kissed the backs of my hands and released me. "I'm a creature of pleasure, Randy. Especially in my human form. I have experienced many things. I know how flesh calls to flesh. With Gareth, I also understand there is a deeper connection. His aura calls to you. I can see it when you are together."

"It's his aura, the calm I feel around him?"

"Yes. He soothes something in your own aura, like a soft light for the shadow. Whereas I add to your shadows. Give you depth. Help you explore the dark. As much as I am connected to you, I also know Gareth is connected to you. This means you need not worry, Randy." He threw in a feline grin and said, "I can share."

I swallowed. Hard. Images flashed through my mind, of me and Ny and Gareth, sending sparks straight to my core. A soft purr slipped from Ny, as if he sensed it or even knew what I was thinking. Sharing was caring, after all.

Shaking my head, I said, "Okay, okay. You and I and Gareth are on the same page. I care for you both. Don't blame me for wanting to be sure everyone is okay with all this." I waved my hand feebly, as if the silly gesture could encompass all we'd experienced.

Ny leaned back, his arm flung over the back of his chair, all cool-dude grace. "I'm more than okay, Randy."

I snorted. "Of course you are."

"So are you." It wasn't a lie. "However, you may not be okay with me for long." He stood to take our now-empty plates to the kitchen. Over his shoulder, he said, "We need to practice shadow walking again. Tonight."

He was right. I wasn't okay with him after his announcement.

# Twenty-One

I WASN'T HAPPY ABOUT it, grumbled and snarked a whole lot, but I did the shadow-walking training. It took a lot of mental effort to make myself come apart. For some stupid reason, I hadn't considered the physicality of coming apart first. My magic, my mind... getting in the right headspace to actually pull it off had taken all my attention. Then I'd dissolved into whatever shadows were made of, and it hurt—hurt worse than anything I'd ever felt. I was unmade, in a way, and felt every rending.

I screamed. Agonizing, wrenching screams even to my ears. Ny was frantic, but there was little he could do while I was in transition from one shadow to another. I jumped about ten feet, from the darkened doorway of my bedroom to a shadowed corner of my living room, my scream following like an echo the fraction of a second it took to move across the space.

I managed to come back together with sheer force of will and whatever it was inside me that made me so like shadows. I came together panting, sweating, and cursing. Cursing Ny specifically. He crouched, curling around me, offering soothing caresses on my shuddering back.

"What the hell?" I yelled, more from fear than anger.

"Sweetling. Randy. I am so very sorry. I didn't know. More aptly, I did not consider how it would be different for you."

"It doesn't rip you apart in agonizing pain? How lucky for you."

"My human form is created, partly by my own will. I can make myself any form I wish in this plane. I happen to favor this, the pharaoh. Sentimentality, mainly, as it was one of the first forms I took amongst humans. All this to say, I can change form without consequence. However, you were born to this form. To force yourself into another material or shape is to rend the original. A painful process, indeed, by the look and sound of it. A process I should've considered. For my negligence and lack of foresight, I am deeply sorry, lovely."

"You should be," I hissed, but deflated after my breath became more smooth and mellow, helped along by Ny's gentle touches.

"Sorry I snapped at you, Ny. It wasn't really your fault." It was my fault, or more accurately a fault with who and what I was. Dammit, why did it all have to be so weird and complicated with me?

I sat calmly half in and out of shadow for long minutes, Ny hovering to help or comfort if I needed him to do either. No pain lingered after the fact. I wasn't hurt in any way when I came back to myself. It was still unpleasant to the nth degree. I didn't want to do it again, but I did. Because it might be helpful to me or, more importantly, someone else in the future.

Despite the initial shock of excruciating pain, the more I shadow walked, the less it hurt. Ny confessed he got around town this way. Shadow walking was better than a car for him. Didn't see easy, breezy, shadowy transportation in my future, but he assured me it would be simpler and less painful once my body became used to the transition. It would take time, like everything else. Annoyingly, time was something we didn't have much of, something we desperately needed but couldn't create out of thin air or shadow, so I gritted my teeth and tried to will the pain to pass.

Ny TRIED TO STAY the night, but I nixed his suggestion. I needed to rest and have some alone time. I knew he'd be attuned to me in whatever way he was and would come running like he did the other night when Merry and Mia were here. I'd managed to keep them away too, with multiple threats, then assurances Ny was a blink away. More like a shadow away, but whatever.

I couldn't hold Gareth off, or really didn't think to try. He showed up bright and far too early the next morning. My body was sore from shadow walking and Ny, so I was slow to reach the door. One look at me, and his face was all concern.

"What happened last night? Or is this from Wilbur?" he asked as he pushed me back into the dark stairway leading up to my apartment.

My main problem was I was tired, mentally and physically. Hard to explain, so I shook my head in answer and leaned on the banister as I trudged up my stairs. When we were in my apartment, door closed and the morning light causing a hazy yellow glow in my space, Gareth pulled me close.

"Randy, tell me you're okay."

"Tired. Plus, I did some new, not-much-fun magic training last nights. Effective results, but also majorly shitty in the execution."

He was so damn earnest, so caring, so kind in all ways. A part of me felt bad, even though I knew I shouldn't. I needed to tell him about the other major event of last night, so I reared back to look him in the face and blurted it out without thinking too much about it. "Ny and I had sex last night."

Gareth blinked at me, searching my face for something I couldn't place. "Are you okay?"

"Okay as it relates to the actual sex? Yep. I, you know, wanted you to know."

"Got it," he drawled out slowly. "We discussed this before, Randy. I understand. You don't owe me any explanations."

"Maybe not, but you have a right to know, so now you do."

He shrugged casually, still holding me in his arms, and said, "Now I know."

He kept staring, hazel eyes locked on mine, until they heated around the edges. He licked his lips and quietly asked, "How was it?"

I squirmed in his arms, unsure what he wanted, so I offered my own shrug in return, not saying anything.

Slowly, Gareth walked me back until my back brushed against a clear section of wall in my apartment entry way. His arms moved from around me to beside me, caging me with his big body. A body he leaned down to skim across mine as he gave me a scorching once-over. "Did you enjoy yourself?"

I couldn't not answer, the heat between us opening me up like a present. "Yes," I whispered with a husky note in my voice.

Gareth leaned down to me, his nose skimming my hair, and burrowed farther to hit right above my ear so he could add his own whisper. "I can almost smell him on you, Randy."

My chest heaved as his right hand moved down, gently running from my shoulder to my hand, jumping from there to hip, to stomach, to the tip-top of my loose pajama pants. He stopped, his hand hovering. "May I touch you, Randy?"

"God, yes." I moaned, and he wasted no time. His hand dove right in, past pjs and panties, and hit my tingling clit. I practically jumped out of my skin at the burst of pleasure.

Gareth bore down, switching to use his thumb so he could insert one finger, then two, deep inside me. As he circled and pumped, he kept up his deep whispers. "Did he make you come? Did you moan for him like you do for me?"

A moaned "yes" was my reply, and my hands moved up to claw at his shoulders. I ground my hips into his hand, wanting more. Wanting everything. This was different from last night with Ny. Not nearly as intense, but no less delicious for it. I looked at his arms and registered the flare of sigils and for a second, thought of sex magic, what Gareth and I might create together. How different it would be from what Ny and I had created.

"I'd like to see it," he said, breathy and hot in my ear. "Ny making you scream for him. Before or after I do. I wouldn't be picky, as long as I could feel you underneath me."

The image of the three of us together tipped me over the edge. I buried my face in Gareth's broad chest as I screamed out my release. He saw me through it, then eased back with a satisfied smile.

I straightened myself and pulled Gareth's tattooed left arm my way, studying the hidden swirl of sigils there. "What do you know about sex magic?" I asked.

He cocked his head. "Not much, actually. I've never attempted to use it before. It's a branch of magic I found no need to study."

"Why?"

"It seemed..."

"Unseemly?" I smirked.

"Not exactly," he said. "I'm no prude. Never thought it was necessary to study or undertake in any serious way."

"You've noticed it between us, right? Your sigils flare whenever we do anything sexual. Like they're siphoning magic."

He squirmed at this and said, "Randy, I've never intentionally pulled magic from you."

"Oh, no." I moved to reassure him with a hug. "I don't think you did, Gareth. Maybe whatever it is I feel from you, with you, helps create magic somehow. It happened in a dramatic way with Ny last night, which is why I know more about it now. He explained sex magic a little. Got me thinking about things, that's all."

Gareth hugged me back and asked with a laugh, "Thinking good thoughts?"

"Maybe having sex magic in our back pocket wouldn't be such a bad thing." It was half a joke, really. It could come in handy one day. As a bonus, practicing for such a day would be a whole lot more fun than my normal magic practice.

# TWENTY-TWO

NATE WAS A WEEK on the job and already a lifesaver. I was slammed with business and magic, the magic more pressing because of the very real danger of Wilbur slinking back around to do whatever it was he had planned. Didn't mean I could stop paying bills and running a business to pay those bills. I'd be a frantic mess if Nate hadn't come along. He had a cool efficiency in the kitchen, and I already trusted him to take over all my standard bakes. I'd thankfully cut back on taking special orders the last few weeks because I'd been too busy. Past Randy had really done me a favor there. Past Merry was owed a big old kiss for sending this awesome young baker my way. I was also sure he had magical affinity. Ny had confirmed it after their brief meeting. Still didn't know if he knew, and I really didn't want to be the one to tell him, so I left that can of worms alone. I needed him on cookie and cupcake duty for now. I'd handle the magic stuff.

Or attempt to handle the magic stuff. If I lived in an eighties' movie, it would be training montage time.

Sadly, I hadn't learned a handy spell for time manipulation. What I did do was put in hours and hours and hours every day with Ny. We shadow walked, so I could move from room to room if I knew the layout of each. The pain became more manageable, more like a split second of one limb being ripped off instead of my entire body imploding slowly. So, progress there.

Ny was good with weapons too, so we worked the spear. Gareth again took some PTO and started doing training with us on the meditation-kitchen plane. It was surprisingly easy for the three of us to connect there and practice fighting, spells, whatever.

Still, I was on a time crunch, and we needed more information to move forward in a tangible way. We knew a lot about Macy, Wilbur, and Starry Wisdom. What we didn't know were biggies—like what they had planned and where, exactly, they were lying low. I needed to know more about the location of the creepy dream house, and I thought I had a good plan to get the info.

"NOT A GOOD IDEA," Gareth said in a firm voice, his arms folded across his chest and his feet planted.

"Why? Because there's an actual issue or do you not want me to do it?" I was pushing back. If there was a real reason I shouldn't, I wanted to know. If he was being overprotective, he could shove it.

The plan I'd come up with was to dream walk to the creepy house on my own then make my way outside the house to find clues to its actual location. I knew how it felt to be there, knew a lot of what it looked like, had been pulled there against my will. Figured I could get there if I tried.

"There's too much we don't know," Gareth said.

"True..." Ny slid into the conversation from his lounging position on my couch.

I glared and didn't let him finish. "Look, I know it's not perfect, but we need to move the needle somehow. We can't risk sitting around waiting for them to do something."

Ny rolled his eyes my way. "I was about to agree with you, Randy."

"Oh, well. Okay then."

Gareth grumbled something about stubbornness but didn't add anything else.

"You do, however, need to take several precautions. We do this in full daylight with Merry present, as well as Gareth and me by your side."

"I'm cool with that. Let's call Merry."

"You want to do this now?" Gareth asked, incredulous.

"It's noon. We're burning daylight. Burning days, in fact. We have to do something and do it quickly."

He sighed a big, put-out sigh but agreed. I gave him a hug to offer a little comfort, which worked some. He didn't have to exactly like the plan, but I wanted him on my side. I even told him as much.

"I'm always on your side, Randy," he said with a tight squeeze.

"Thanks." I smiled back. "And I'll be safe. Scout's honor."

He snorted, likely because he guessed right. I'd never been any kind of scout.

"Enough cuddling... unless you're willing to let me participate," Ny said as he rose from the couch.

I snorted but moved from Gareth's arms, calling Merry to tell her the plan. She jumped at the opportunity to help, like always, and strolled through my door thirty minutes later, with Harley in tow.

"Hope you don't mind me crashing your party," she said flatly.

"More the merrier," I said with a wink at Merry, who groaned at the old joke I used to make of her name.

She swatted at me with her hand. "Let's get this done."

"Thanks for taking off for this. I know the shelter is busy."

"They're flexible, so no worries."

"My schedule is fairly open, in case you were wondering," Harley said.

"Yeah. Secret occultist brokers can make their own schedules, I suppose," I replied with a snort. Harley merely shook her head and slid up next to Merry, taking her lithe frame in a side-arm hug.

I was ready to get this over with, so I corralled everyone into my bedroom. Then I pushed everyone out, because it was super weird to try to sleep with a bunch of people staring at me. Eventually, Ny and Gareth came in to help me meditate some, calm me down. Maybe they added a little extra mojo in there, too; one minute I thought I'd never fall asleep, then then next I was standing in the foyer of the crappy old house.

It was still daytime. Shafts of sunlight shifted through seriously dingy windows situated to the side of the front door. I stood motionless for a solid minute, listening as hard as I could. Straining to hear even the smallest sound. I heard nothing, so I moved, noticing I was once again in my odd black-robe attire. Why I couldn't dream walk in jeans and a tee I didn't know, but I had other concerns. Like getting out the door and having a real look around the neighborhood.

When I got to the door, it wouldn't open. Not for me anyway. The wood was regular old wood. I could slip through it maybe an inch, but something like a wall met me on the other side. Not enough to poke my head out for a look around. The barrier had for sure not been there before. Some new defensive spells put into place more than likely. Possibly because of my last stunt when pulled into the house. I had to work around it somehow.

I tried opening the door, but no luck there, either. First, it took way too much time and concentration to get my hand to not slide right through the brass doorknob. Once I could grasp it, I discovered the door didn't budge anyway, as if locked in place by something other than a doorknob.

I knew there was big magic here. Felt it all around. Saw traces of sigils and other things. I'm sure one of them held the door fast for any number of reasons. I wasn't well-read enough in sigils to be able to pinpoint which one did it, and I didn't have time to try to wipe them all out. I'd already wasted too much time. Seemed the windows were my only option.

I was tired of trying to force my body to have effect in the real world, so I called DD to me. It sped right to me at my call, ready to do whatever I needed. At the moment, I needed a window washer. DD scrubbed in short bursts at one of the windows, creating an eye-level view out of the dingy thing. Outside I saw the porch, the broken concrete and sidewalk, the warped fence. I bent and craned for more, seeing other houses and cars for the first time, but none of it gave me a clue. After contorting for a while, I got the right angle. I caught sight of a cross street a few houses down, and with a squint, I made out the street signs in the bright light of day. Mt. Vernon and Champion. An actual location.

I whooped in celebration without thinking, then clamped a hand over my mouth as if I could somehow shove the sound back in there. My internal cursing at myself gave me time and silence enough to hear the frenzied scurrying of tiny paws my way.

John the rat-man familiar came barreling down the stairs, right at me. He jumped, attempting to land on me to do serious damage, but couldn't. I was dream walking here on my terms and had no real substance unless I wanted to have it. I definitely didn't want a rat thing feeling my substance, so it met nothing but air. A half squeal, half growl of frustration came from the creature as it shook off its hard landing. It closed its human eyes, and the fur along its body rippled as if something under its skin moved and stretched. It flashed with some inner light, like a sigil, and crouched with a hiss before sprinting back my way.

It stuck when it hit this time. Maybe from the residual effect of what it was able to do last time or something else. Didn't really have time to think through the magical logistics as it clawed its way up my body, its weight getting heavier as it climbed. It was about to settle on me like before, stick me to place, but I grabbed its squirming body in my hands and threw it like a football up onto the stairs. It hit with a loud thump before it made an angry racket.

Its half scream, half squeal of outrage woke something upstairs. Something with the power to do more damage. I heard the shuffling of feet across old floors and knew my time was about up. I needed to get out, get away, but I needed focus and calm to do it effectively. Merry had always pulled me out; I hadn't called on her to do it. It was the same idea in theory, but trying to pull it off in practice with a rat-man screaming was something else entirely.

John wouldn't stop and was already down the stairs and nearly at my feet once again. Whatever was upstairs flung a door open, and I knew I had seconds to get clear. Without conscious thought, my spear popped into my hand. I took aim and slid it right through the squirming body of John the rat-man. He yelled, far more human than rat in the sound. A thundering scream echoed from above a split second later. I'd pissed someone off up there, and it was time to go.

I flung rat blood from my spear, closed my eyes as the sound of footsteps grew closer, and raced for the old telephone in my mind. I'd barely had it off the cradle before screaming for Merry to pick up, pick up, pick up. I felt a whoosh, as if something ran toward me, and the scratch of nails on my arms, then I bolted up in bed. Merry was holding tight to me. I looked down at the nail marks clawed into my flesh, blood dripping onto my bed.

"That was close," I said in a rush, my breathing heavy.

"Too close," Ny said with a dark look my way.

"Doesn't matter, because I know where the house is." I didn't smile, didn't gloat. I got up to get some alcohol and a bandage and get Mia on the line. This shit had to end. ASAP.

# TWENTY-THREE

MERRY TOOK THE INITIATIVE to call Mia over, as I was in a daze. My plan had actually worked but had resulted in blood—thankfully not too much of my own. With a few big splashes of cold water on my face and a solid minute-long stare at myself in the mirror, I snapped out of it. I didn't have time to think on it, but the questions still bubbled up anyway. What was I becoming?

I knew I had done what I had to do, for my family, my friends, my city, and myself. Hell, maybe for the world. I'd been lucky enough to push aside what I did to Macy at the church and to have that—for good and bad—not be permanent. John's blood was on my hands, no doubt. I saw its life fade at the end of my spear. Maybe I shouldn't care. It was a familiar, not really an animal or a human. Not really anything but a tool for Macy's use. Still, I knew the look on its face would stay with me, even as I pushed it aside. Even as I knew I'd probably have to spill more blood before all this was over. At least I felt bad about today. I dreaded the possibility one day I wouldn't care.

Harley knocked hard on the bathroom door. "Mia's here."

Mia sat slouched over her laptop already, giving me a not-very-jaunty wave as she focused in on her screen. I hadn't seen her for a week, and she looked like she hadn't slept the whole time. Whatever was up with her was taking a toll, and I didn't like it. Before I could ask or nag, she flipped her laptop around to show everyone.

"A database of some sort?" I asked.

"Not just any database. It's the Necronomicon digitally organized in database form. I'm at about ninety-five percent compilation. Don't know if the other five percent is accessible or feasible. What I do have gives us a lot of solid info. And spells. A shit ton of spells."

Harley plopped down by my sister without speaking, scrolling through the database at a steady clip. Her eyes grew wider the longer she scrolled, until she leaned back in her chair and let out a harsh breath. "Damn" was all she said at first. Shaking her head free of the shock or amazement or mixture of both, she looked to Ny. "Might be best you have a look too. Some of this is beyond my experience. What's not is still on par with the most complex spells I've encountered."

Ny nodded in agreement but didn't move forward. "The Necronomicon is best kept in human hands," he said in a stilted manner.

"You won't help them?" I asked.

"I shouldn't help."

"Is it safe for them?" I asked Ny, gesturing to Mia and Harley.

"There is danger. Some spells and knowledge could be traced back to them. Potentially, they could be exposed to any number of practitioners. There is no way to know."

"Sounds like not a great idea," Merry said, looking between her sister and her girlfriend with worry.

"I've used sections of the Necronomicon before," Harley said, offering Merry a reassuring look. "Gareth has as well. Most mages worth their salt have studied fragments to some extent. I know of sections I can use safely and securely. Spells with power and force which have little chance of tracing back to us."

"Do we absolutely need those spells?" I asked.

Gareth joined the conversation, saying, "We might, Randy. Especially if you now plan to attack the house, and by extension, Macy and Wilbur."

Wilbur. I'd pushed him to the back of my mind, but if the creepy-ass house was where Macy hung out, Wilbur was probably also a big part of what went down there. He was her master, or as close to it as we could figure. I wasn't jumping up and down to go toe-to-toe with him again. To be honest, I didn't like my odds. The

Necronomicon might give an edge, and against Wilbur any advantage could mean a whole lot.

"I don't like it," I said on a huff, "but we need the extra oomph. I also trust you all to stay safe."

"I'll get the other five percent. Somehow," Mia muttered.

"Nope. Nuh-uh. What we have is good. You're off this thing."

"What do you mean?" she asked, looking genuinely confused. I scoffed then threw my arms out, waving them up and down at her.

"Have you seen yourself lately?" I practically yelled. She flinched then rallied. "Not nice, sis."

"What'd be not nice would be me letting you do whatever it is you're doing to yourself for my own selfish reasons."

Gareth was quiet and calm when he stepped into the fray to say, "Mia, honey, Randy's right."

Merry gave her no quarter either. "This stops. Now."

Mia looked at Harley, but if she expected support from her, she was sorely mistaken. "We're good, Mia. You obviously aren't. This has to stop."

"Mia," Ny said, snagging her tired eyes with his starry ones. "All can see you love your sister. You've done an excellent job giving us tools to protect her. Show yourself the same love."

Mia couldn't hold out against all of us. She deflated even more, shook her head, and muttered, "Fine. I'll show Harley everything I have and leave it alone."

Harley gave silent confirmation. If nothing else, I knew Harley would pull Mia back if it was necessary. She'd do all she could to keep both my sisters safe, for a variety of reasons all her own, so I let the matter go for the time being.

"Okay then. I have a location. From GPS, it looks to be over off Broad, not far from Franklin Conservatory. It was on a street with other houses, so we need to be careful. Crossfire wouldn't be good."

"Agreed," Gareth said. "It might be best to go on a weekday afternoon. Less likely to have others around."

"One spell I know we can use from the book is a powerful isolation spell. It separates a place from its surroundings by way of a magical barrier. It will make it so others are less likely to get hurt. Also locks in inhabitants so they can't flee. Whoever is inside the space when the spell clicks into place will be forced to stay there, no matter what."

"We'll be able to come and go?" I asked.

"Yes," Harley assured me. "As long as you're outside the spell's perimeter when it's cast, you'll be good."

"Fab. I'll be happy to see how they like being trapped in their creepy-ass house. What do you need to pull it off?"

"I'll need to be in a secure location. I'll need someone else at the house to help complete the spell."

"I'll do it," Gareth called, stepping up.

"Cool, cool," I said, a bit distracted. A plan was taking form in my mind, so I let it out. "This is what

I'm thinking. Mia, Merry, and Harley—you all stay at Harley's place. It's warded out the wazoo, so you should be good in terms of protection."

The ladies agreed, so I kept with my spontaneous planning. "Gareth, you go to the house to help Harley complete her spell. Then you stay outside as backup. Can you handle that? Stay outside unless you're needed? Not be a part of physically taking Wilbur down?"

A muscle ticked in his jaw. It pained him, the idea of letting us do something he'd thought of doing for so many years. Letting us take on his revenge. But Gareth was not only a good man, he was a smart man. He slashed his head down in agreement. He'd do what needed to be done to get Wilbur, including letting someone else do the actual getting.

"Ny and I will shadow walk inside the place. A surprise invasion."

"Can you take down Macy and Wilbur?" Harley asked us.

"I got Macy. Don't worry about it," I said, the sting of her claw marks searing at the thought of all the threats she'd flung at my sisters.

"I'm prepared for Wilbur now. Know his tricks. He shouldn't be a problem," Ny said with a flippant confidence.

I turned to Merry. "I'm not dream walking, so I won't need your anchor. But stay close and alert just in case. Who knows what might happen or what tricks we may need to pull off."

"To be perfectly clear," Mia said, piping in. "What is the objective of all this?"

I shrugged and said, "Simple. Take out Wilbur and Macy. With them gone, no more dream walking nightmares and no more Starry Wisdom. Easy peasy."

"Are you okay with might happen there? What you might have to do?" Merry asked, concern clear in her voice and her face.

"Maybe. Maybe not. Don't really have a choice in the matter. Wilbur made it clear he wanted to use me for something. Starry Wisdom already tried to grab me. They all know who I care about and what I'd do for them. At this point, it's them or us. And I choose us. I'll deal with the fallout another day."

Merry's eyes glistened as if she'd cry but she pulled herself up, shook her head, and gave a wonky smile my way. "We'll deal with whatever we have to later. Together."

Ny said nothing but brushed up against my side. Gareth moved close as well. Harley and Mia, still sitting at the table, offered their own assurances. All of them were there because of me—because they wanted to help me. "Right," I said, strong and clear. My stomach twisted in worry and fear, but they didn't need to see it. "Let's do this damn thing."

WE GAVE OURSELVES TWO days, landing us firmly in midweek. Harley and Gareth studied the spell they intended to use. Gareth went out in stealth mode during daylight hours to put a number of sigils down for the spell to work and study the new spells I encountered when I last dream walked there. He came back confident he'd set everything up in our favor. Hopefully none of his work was spotted or manipulated before we attacked.

Ny helped me practice shadow walking so we could slip into the house once the isolation spell slammed down on it. I hurt less and could go farther with each jump. It was exhausting, painful, annoying work, but I did it. It was the best weapon I had, mainly because no one outside the group knew I had it. Surprise was key to us getting the upper hand, and me being able to move through shadows at will was one hell of a surprise.

Mia grumbled about having nothing to do and, at one point, resorted to thoroughly cleaning her guns in front of everyone. "Just in case," she said as she scoured the dismantled handgun with an old toothbrush like she was cleaning tile grout, a tip she'd claimed came from Gareth. Merry balked and fussed at her. I said nothing because, secretly, I was glad. Any extra bit of protection was good. Also, I was happy Gareth was helping my sisters in every way they could be helped.

"Magic can do a lot, but bullets have their uses," he said in his soft grumble. Had to agree with him, in theory at least.

Ny slid beside me as I leaned against my bedroom door, watching Merry and Mia bicker late in the night before our planned attack. "The more time I spend with you and your sisters, the more jealous I become," he said in a serious, quiet voice.

"What? Why?" I asked. Why would an Outer God ever be jealous of the Carters? We were a bit of a mess.

"The care. The concern. The love. Believe me, not all family dynamics function the same way."

"Ny," I said, pulling him into the darkness of my bedroom for more privacy. "Wilbur is your nephew, right? Damn, I didn't even think of that. Are you really okay with the plan?"

He leaned his head down so his forehead met mine. "My sweet Randy. As I said, not all family dynamics mirror what you have with your sisters. Part of me may feel remorse for what must be done, yet it must be done because of Wilbur's own actions, possibly the actions of his father. Where I'm from, such actions have swift and sure consequences."

"Doesn't make it any fun," I muttered.

"No, sweetling. I can think of far more pleasurable things to do with you," he said with a gruff laugh. He pushed back to look down at me, his starry eyes clashing with my navy gaze. "Thank you, lovely, for asking. For your concern." He brought a hand to my cheek and held me there in his palm, the magical energy a zipping crackle between us. "So sweet, in taste and temperament," he whispered.

"I can be very bitter too, Ny."

"I don't doubt it," he said, stepping away, leaving me to think about how bitter I might need to be the following day.

# Twenty-Four

WE STARTED EARLY THE day of, helping Harley and Gareth prep for the isolation spell. Hitting the house around one in the afternoon worked best—less likely to be any people, adults or kids, around at that time on a random weekday. I figured we needed no more than an hour. Honestly, much longer and things weren't going to go in our favor. We had Ny and most of the Necronomicon helping us, but surprise and what a forties black-and-white movie might call gumption were the traits working in our favor most. We lost those, our odds plummeted.

Harley, Merry, and Mia posted up at Harley's place. Gareth and I went over briefly. I was there to help however I could, but really, there wasn't much for me to do in terms of the spell. Harley and Gareth had it covered, or as covered as they could. I trusted them both to get it done. Each had proven numerous times already they knew their shit, so I left them to it. Not much else I could give them beyond a pep talk they didn't need.

What I could do, in the early hours of the morning, was hang with my sisters. Check on them. Mia was still brassed off about the whole Necronomicon thing, but I didn't care if it made her mad. She sported harsh bluish-purple half-moons under her eyes and walked more hunched, more cautious, than normal. Her hair looked a few days past wash day. I wasn't one to judge, but Mia was usually super serious about styling her short, dark hair on the daily. Not high maintenance in any other way, but her hair was something she enjoyed spending time on, so neglecting it was a bad sign. Whatever the search for the book had done to her, it wasn't good.

Merry saw it all, too, and also worried for the baby of the family. She tried to get her to talk about what the search was like, why she was going through this odd transformation in front of our eyes, but no luck. Mia sulked and remained tight-lipped. I'd lectured her again the night before about how I didn't need this book she was so determined to give me. Maybe she'd listened. Maybe not.

I wouldn't lecture her again. This time before my battle was for something else. "Would Harley be cool with me using her kitchen?" I asked Merry in a hushed voice. Harley and Gareth were huddled in one corner of the office, or fighting floor, of Harley's place, and us Carters stood around twiddling our thumbs at the other end.

"If you're making something good for all of us, then yes, it's fine," Harley yelled, somehow hearing my questions.

"Didn't know, seeing as I've never even seen your kitchen."

She gave a snort-laugh in reply and quipped, "Rarely see it myself."

Merry shook her head at our back and forth and tugged on my arm. "Come on. I'll show you where it is."

When I slung my reusable grocery sack over my shoulder—there was more than one way to help save the world and all—Mia perked up slightly. "Whatcha got in there?"

"Come with us and find out," I answered, holding my hand out to her. She hesitated but took it, giving it an affectionate squeeze for good measure as we trooped up the stairs to Harley's living space.

I was disappointed to see it was much the same as all the other parts of Harley's place I'd seen. New, shiny, high-end, and not very personal. At least not in the hallway or open kitchen-living room combo I'd looked over. Two exceptions jumped out at me. The first was a framed picture in her hallway. The frame was thick, dark wood, polished to a high shine. It was one of those big square ones with the photo in the middle expertly matted and preserved. The photo in question was old, squat and square like home photos from the '50s or '60s often were, the white border of the actual image turned slightly yellow from time. Smack in the middle of the square was a smiling family: a large Black man with astute, dark eyes and a winning smile, a beautiful and poised Black woman with Harley's bone structure, and a mini-Harley in braids grinning between the two. It was her family, a beautifully preserved picture of people she'd loved and lost. It tugged at my heart, both to imagine the loss and see the reverence she'd put into keeping this image with her.

The second was in the kitchen itself, and maybe someone who wasn't me wouldn't have noticed it. Right in the middle of Harley's sleek and meticulously clean kitchen, two dirty coffee mugs sat on the counter. The dirty coffee mugs weren't a surprise. It was early and all. The mugs themselves were what put a goofy grin on my face. Both were black with a graphic of an old-school name tag, except the name tags were rainbow colored. In cursive print they read, "Hello! Ask me about my gay agenda." Those were from Merry, I was 100 percent sure. She had a thing for novelty coffee mugs and gave them to people all the time. I had at least half a dozen from her in my kitchen, all baking themed in some way. Same with Mia and our parents, Mia's with computer nerd things and my parents with mom or dad puns.

"Cute mugs," I said with a sly grin.

Merry waved at a stacking set of stark-white mugs by a coffee machine. "Ugh. She had these," she replied with disdain.

"The horror!" I said with faux shock, which made Mia laugh. It felt good, the teasing and laughing. I wanted to spend this time with my sisters, feed them and talk to them. Because what if? But also because it grounded me in a way little else did.

"Who's up for buckwheat pancakes with strawberries?" I asked the room, which made Mia perk up even more. Good.

"Yes, please," she said, taking a seat on a high stool in Harley's kitchen. Merry emphatically shook her head yes and sat down too. They knew not to offer to help. I didn't need it. Didn't want it. Not in this. The cooking would give me focus and calm. As would the chat and the occasional laughter. If there was a note of desperation there, sadness, something unknown and uncertain, that was okay. We did the best we could with what we had and what we all guessed could happen real soon.

AFTER TASTY PANCAKES AND some heavy good-byes we tried to not make heavy, I crawled onto the back of Gareth's bike and clung to his warmth as we zipped through the noon streets of Columbus. His calming aura was dampened, much like it had been the night before our fight at the black church. No time to give him the same comfort I had given him then, unless I wanted to strip in the middle of the street. What I could give was a strong hold on his taut body, pressing firmly against him as we moved at dizzying speeds.

He parked about two blocks away from the cross street. Ny stood, loose and waiting, in the designated spot. Gareth and I took off our helmets and squinted in the bright summer light over at the Outer God. He looked fine, in more ways than one. Looked human, if one didn't stare too closely at his shadow, which was a little too long, a little too writhing, to be perfectly natural. Gareth opened his mouth to say something, but I stopped him. Reaching up on my tiptoes, I planted a soft, sweet kiss on his mouth. "Not now," I said as I pulled back. I was firm, resolute, and assuring when I added "later."

His hazel eyes flashed more green than brown in the sunlight. I knew he'd do what he had to do to give us another time, another day, to talk again.

We reached Ny and, without a word, moved as a group toward the old house. I'd never seen the outside in real life, or in daylight. It was even worse from this perspective. Nothing but rotted wood, peeling paint, and grimy windows—a broken thing giving off the scent of decay. A regular person might smell it and think it came from the house, but I'd gotten a big old whiff of Wilbur before and knew the wretched mix of rotted things and spoiled dirt came from him.

Gareth went to check all the sigils and counter spells were in place as Ny and I stood a few houses down, waiting.

"Are you ready, Randy?"

"As ready as I'll ever be, I guess."

Ny turned serious, his night-sky eyes looking out of place in the summer daylight. "I will do all I can to protect you."

"I know that." I did. Didn't know how I was so certain of it, but I was. Ny would help me, whatever the cost. "Hoping I won't need protecting, but thanks."

Ny laughed. "Oh, sweetling. You are endlessly amusing." He dipped down and said, "Do I also get a soft, lingering kiss?"

"Why not?" I answered and leaned against his hard body. I paused for a moment, studying the planes and lines of his tawny face. "All jokes aside, Ny. Thanks for helping with this. For going in there with me."

"We have a common goal," he said with courteous nonchalance, but I didn't fully believe it. Not with the lingering look in his eyes, the way his body felt as I curled into him. The heat and magic surrounding us. He'd be here, regardless of his missing book or powers. If he knew I was here. I didn't tell him I suspected as much. Instead, I pressed up, softly caressing his lips with mine, willing my magic, my essence, and my aura or whatever it could be called to help express the idea for me. Gareth came back as Ny held me in his arms, midnight eyes blinking down at me with what I

imagined was a little bit of awe, and told us we were
good to go.

# Twenty-Five

GARETH POSITIONED HIMSELF AT the apex of the sigil markers, shaking out his limbs slightly and breathing deep. He usually felt so calm to me, so it was odd to see him show small signs of nerves. I wanted to help him, give him some calm, but in reality I didn't have any to give. He was the one usually giving it to me, and it was shitty I couldn't return the favor. As if he somehow knew the direction of my thoughts, he squinted those hazel eyes of his my way and gave a small grin as a sign he was all good. I didn't buy it, but I blew him a kiss.

He stood almost directly in front of the house in the middle of the street. It was a tiny side street, so not much traffic on a weekday afternoon. Still, Ny and I kept watch for cars. Wouldn't help matters if someone plowed into Gareth as he worked a spell.

For a minute that felt like an eternity, Gareth stood straight and tall, at first glance looking like he wasn't doing much of anything. His head dangled forward, loose and ready. His arms were tense at his sides. I

could barely see it, but his lips moved slowly, deliber-
ately, forming words I couldn't catch from my distance
a few houses down.

Then, his arms started to glow along the edges of his
sigil tattoos. The light amped up in seconds, flaring
bright and strong through the glare of the summer
sun. When they shimmered like a mirage, he flung his
hands out in front of him, straight at the creepy-ass
house, and roared something I couldn't understand.
Magic flung out, firing the sigils around the house so
they sizzled–some disappearing, some strengthening.
An invisible wall of power slammed down around the
house, connecting sigil to sigil, leaving no space or
crack for whatever happened inside the walls to leak
out to the street.

Gareth sagged, as if completely exhausted from the
spell. He likely was. The level of power he'd thrown
out was enough to make my magic thrum and my skin
prickle from yards away. Ny and I moved toward him
as soon as the last piece clicked into place, but I ran
forward when he took a knee, unable to hold himself
standing any longer.

"Gareth!" I skidded to a stop on my knees, ignoring
the slice of asphalt through my dark jeans, and lifted
his chin up so I could meet his eyes.

"I'm fine," he croaked. He didn't look fine. He looked
drained, his color flat and pale, his eyes not nearly as
bright as usual.

"Bullshit," I whispered, running my hand along his hair to get the loosened blond strands out of his face. "We need to get you out of here."

"No," he said, a firmness coming into his face. "No way."

"We do not have time, Randy," Ny said.

"We'll make time!" I yelled.

He bent down, laying a hand on my shoulder. "Sweetling, let me help him."

"You can?"

"I'm an Outer God. Of course I can," he said with his cocky air. He shooed me to the side and knelt in front of Gareth, who held up a shaking hand in front of himself.

"How much will this drain you?" he asked. "You'll need all your power to fight Wilbur."

Ny shrugged. "I'm confident we have enough."

I chewed my lip, now concerned for everyone. Gareth needed help, but we needed power. And we all needed to get this done quickly or else the surprise element was out the grimy window.

I started to say something. Gareth did too. Ny was having none of our human hedging. He simply grabbed Gareth's forearms in a painful-looking grip as the whites of his eyes disappeared, turning into the swirling, roiling black I'd seen when we'd had sex, like it was a small glimpse into the chasm of power his human form contained. He stared straight into Gareth, who was transfixed by Ny's gaze. His sigils flared as a crackle of Ny's power rose between the two men. Ny was giving him magic, jump-starting his battery in some way.

Eventually, Ny loosened his hold on Gareth, who sagged against the Prince. Ny patted his back with what might be affection and whispered something to him I didn't catch. Gareth nodded and pulled himself straight. His forearms flexed as his sigils shimmered, doing whatever work they could do. Which must be a lot, because his color and body language was already better.

"I'm good, Randy," he said as he seemed to test out the returning strength of his body. "Will be better in a matter of minutes. Now go."

I went in for a swift, firm kiss on his lips. Ny held a hand out to help me rise, and we looked down at Gareth as I said, "BRB," trying to defuse the situation. The joke fell flat, but what could I expect? It wasn't a jokey time. Gareth worked his jaw. The best thing I could do for him, for all of us, was stick to the plan. Breaking Gareth's gaze as I turned, I gripped Ny's hand firmly in my own and said, "Time to go for a little walk."

PAIN SEARED ACROSS MY flesh as I became shadow then remade myself. It was so much better than it had been before. Didn't mean it was pleasant.

A handy skill, regardless. It took a split second for Ny and me to move from the open, empty street to the dingy, dusty, dimly lit foyer of the house. Wasn't dimly lit enough to hide the bloodstains from John still streaked across the floor. I shook the thought off as best I could. Closed my eyes, breathed deep, and found my focus so I could do what needed to be done. After. After was when I'd think about it all.

I called DD to me, and it zipped around my head until I called for part of it to take spear form. It did what I asked with little effort on my part. Some of it hovered around me, ready to shield when necessary, but I gripped the writhing shadow weapon in my hand as Ny motioned for us to proceed.

We took the rickety stairs as lightly as we could, but it was an old, rundown house, so it wasn't silent. I directed Ny toward the equation room at the end of the hallway with the weird crack in it. It'd felt powerful, so I figured it might be where Wilbur and Macy did whatever it was they did in this place. On a soft count of three, Ny eased the door open and we moved in, cautious and fully on guard.

No one was there. When I paused to consider it, the place looked, sounded, and felt totally empty. The glowy sigil-like equations were there. I spun to ask Ny what where we should check next, and I saw him frozen in place, staring intently at the walls.

"What's wrong?" I hissed.

"I suspected when you told me, but I couldn't be sure until I saw them." He swallowed, as if he were afraid, and whispered, "Randy, these are no mere sigils or equations. These markings are access keys."

"Access keys to what?" I asked in a hushed voice, trying to be quiet even though my stress was ramping up by the second. Keys unlocked things. The types of things Wilbur and Macy might want to unlock were not good things.

"The Dreamlands." He moved closer to the side wall to gently rub a lifted symbol. "Home."

All I knew of Ny's home was it was a place of powerful nightmares, so I wasn't happy to hear him say it.

We didn't get a chance to discuss more. Ny's head whipped around and stared at the ominous dark crack on the far wall. "Something is coming," he said, moving to step in front of me.

Didn't like his use of the term "something" or his move to shield me. I had my own handy shield, so I stepped to his side and threw up DD as a block between us both. It shook, and I didn't know if DD was scared itself or feeling the effects of my fear. It was scary shit either way.

The crack oozed out the same dark shadow from before. It trembled, elongated, and widened as an eerie deep-blue light pushed through. Withered, old, feminine hands peeled back the wall, and Macy emerged like she were parting a curtain. She looked Ny and me up and down, pure hate burning like dry ice in her cold eyes, but she said nothing to us as she stepped free of the crack and moved quickly to the side. Wilbur came through right on her heels, hunched over for a moment, his steps hard and abrupt.

He surveyed the two of us with a sneer as dark, slithering shadows made smacking noises against the wall and floor. They writhed, wanting to gain hold. Of the room or us, I couldn't be sure, and I wasn't too keen on finding out.

"When I felt the feeble magic surrounding my home, I knew it had to be you," Wilbur spit out coldly.

Ny returned his sneer and his cold tone. "I'm not the one who resorted to years of material manipulation in an attempt to enter the Dreamlands. Couldn't wait to see Daddy, Wilbur?"

"My father can rot, for all I care." He stopped himself from saying more. A gleam shone in Ny's eyes, as if Wilbur had given too much away, and the man saw it.

Macy, all the while, eyed me with her cold, haughty hate. She didn't interrupt her master, but when he stopped speaking, she pounced. "You killed John," she hissed.

Ny took his eyes off Wilbur for a split second to look at me. He didn't look shocked or horrified, more like he wondered why I didn't tell everyone about the rat-man. I hadn't wanted to talk about it, simply as that, but now I wished I'd said something before our attack so it wasn't the witch letting it slip. He should've heard it first from me.

Still, I didn't reply to Macy's statement. No need to say anything. I'd done it. I'd do it again to save myself, but I couldn't joke about it or goad her with it. Something she had no problems with.

"We'll end you all," she said. "Slowly."

"You got the power to actually pull it off?" I asked before slamming the end of my spear down hard on the floor, shadows skittering in its wake. Even the darker, unknown shadows flickered. Interesting, and very possibly useful.

"Yes, girl," she said, her sickeningly sweet, needling tone back in place. "You'll be stripped of all your power because you deserve none. You'll watch, helpless, as those you care for are killed, but not all. You'll see your lovely sister Merry my new familiar. It's hard to manipulate a human into such a thing, but we will soon have all the power we need from—"

Out of nowhere, in the middle of her villain tirade, Wilbur punched Macy right in the face, the heavy thud of fist meeting flesh echoing in the room. "Enough!" he screamed at her.

She cowered back, blood leaking from her mouth. A part of me felt sorry for her. Wondered what her life had been before she turned to magic, became a witch, met Wilbur. Wondered if it was Wilbur who'd led her all along or if she'd found her way to him. None of it excused or justified decades of death and destruction. It might offer some kind of understanding if I thought on it long enough. Didn't have long enough in the moment, so I pushed the thoughts away and refocused. Whatever she was or whyever she was didn't matter. What mattered was what she'd do if she left this house alive, and I wouldn't let that happen. Not while I still lived.

Wilbur seethed, breathing heavy and hard as he turned back to us with clenched fists. "Enough from you as well," he said, raising his hands as his power cascaded over the room. It made my body tremble, my thrum scream, but I stayed standing, unyielding, facing it. I held out for a few seconds, then Ny's actual lion roar filled the room, vibrating the space with his frequency, a frequency providing strength and comfort when I needed the reassurance. I saw Macy cringe back, but Wilbur smiled.

"I will surely enjoy ripping you apart, Nyarlathotep," he said in an almost cheerful voice before he charged us.

# TWENTY-SIX

WILBUR BARRELED INTO NY, knocking him off his feet and clear out of the room. DD hadn't been able to stop him, and he'd ripped through the shield with no problem at all. Luckily, DD rallied and came back together to help me face Macy. Ny could handle himself, so I needed to worry about what was immediately in front of me.

She twisted her neck, as if trying to crack it. Her brittle frame looked like it might keel over if she cracked anything, but I wasn't fooled by those looks. Power radiated off her, making my skin feel buzzed and prickly.

She moved one slow step at a time toward me, dodging the piles of books and discarded artifacts scattered around the room without looking anywhere but straight at me. Her lips were pulled back in a gnashing snarl, yellowed teeth clamped so tight her words slithered out of her.

"You'll regret coming here today. Thinking you were a match for me. For us."

"Us who? Your old ass and disgusting Wilbur? Psht. Please." I crouched in my fight stance, ready for her to pounce as she inched closer and growled at my insults.

"John was with me for centuries," she barked. Blood lingered on her mouth from Wilbur's punch, and she twisted it up in a rage, contorting her already-wrinkled face into something almost not human. "You can't fathom such a connection, what it did to me when you killed him."

"Glad it took a chunk of you with it." I was tired of the talking and ready for the fight. The crashing, snarling, banging noises from the hall, and the waves of power radiating outward from their fight, had me on high alert. If Macy didn't strike soon, I'd have to take the offensive to keep my nerve up in all this building tension.

So quickly I barely tracked her movement, Macy slashed out with her hand, which looked as wicked sharp as any talon. DD shook at the impact but didn't waver. Unlike Wilbur, Macy couldn't easily knock through.

I gripped my spear tighter and gave Macy a grin. "Not as strong as your master, huh?"

"I have no master," she said in the Macy tone I remembered, from when I first met her and she looked young and vital. It didn't matter which form she took, which form was real. Her evil shone through regardless.

Laughing, I shook my head. "Keep telling yourself that, lady. You sold pieces of yourself for power, but all your power came with a price. Masters, controllers, and men on this plane and in others who make you do what they want you to do, when they want you to do it. Servitude seems to be the going rate for pieces of your soul. That and aging not-so-gracefully, by the looks of it."

"We all make sacrifices," she said before bolting forward again to push into DD. The force of her magic and her body fell into us, putting pressure on DD and, by extension, me. My feet nearly tripped up as she pressed us until we fell against a wall, slamming hard into a grouping of glowing equations, which shrank away from my impact. My head snapped to the back and side, hitting the wall hard. I felt a scrape, possibly a trickle of blood, but I ignored it.

I caught my bearings and pushed back, shoving my spear forward. DD let it slip through, and the honed edge of shadow sliced into Macy's shoulder. Ignoring the hit and the blood now trickling down her arm, she focused on the opportunity I gave her and tore into the opening DD made, gripping tight and tearing. There was a wrenching feeling deep in my gut, and I watched as large hunks of DD came off from Macy's now-glowing hands.

"What are you without these shadow games, little girl?" she asked, ripping into DD without remorse. I yelled in frustration but rallied, knowing getting her

was the best way forward, no matter what happened. I
didn't want to sacrifice DD in the process, so I called it
back before it could be too hurt. It resisted for a brief
flash, not wanting to give up its defense of me, but it
did my bidding, as it always did.

When it snapped back to its dense, hovering-ball
form, Macy stutter-stepped, caught off-balance by the
sudden lack of resistance in front of her. It was my turn
to take advantage, and I swept her legs with the butt
of my spear, sending her sprawling to the ground. I
brought the tip down, but she rolled to avoid it, clashing into a stack of books instead of taking the pointy
end of my weapon.

Macy scrambled to duck behind a large trunk
stacked high with old books and I followed, hearing
her mutter some words before I felt a rush of icy-cold
wind rip through me. It froze me in place. I panicked,
screaming in my head with surprise and pain. DD
heard and answered, swooping down to blanket me as
Macy called forward some other spell. The impact of
whatever she flung my way shattered hard across DD,
making the shield waver and go nearly invisible. I felt
my connection to it weaken, as if about to break. My
shock and anger at Macy once again hurting DD pulled
me out of the freeze. It was an odd sensation, like I
shrugged my shoulders and the spell slid away without
much resistance. I had no time to consider it, focusing
on making sure DD was okay.

Macy cackled. "The Deep Dark will learn to distrust you, Miranda. All you seem to do is get it hurt."

I seethed as I stroked down my line, offering as much comfort as I could at the moment. DD was tired, losing power, but unwavering in the spear department. The weight remained heavy in my hand. I murmured down our bond, told it to fall back, rest, and give me the spear and nothing else so it could preserve its energy. It was much quicker to listen this time around, which made me worry more.

Before I could worry too much, Macy was glowing, surely about to throw another spell my way. I stepped back into the small sliver of shadow I felt behind me and instantly transformed. I shadow walked, much to Macy's surprise—if her disbelieving yell was anything to go by—and materialized almost instantly across the room.

"All-new trick," I said as she lunged, her hands crackling with misspent magical energy. Enough to cause real damage if they touched me. I side-stepped her and slipped into another shadow, this time coming back long enough to watch her whirl around toward me again, watching where she headed and the nearest shadow to it.

My blood sang and my flesh ached, shadow walking so many times and so quickly, but I kept it up for the final jump, which brought me directly in front of her before she could register I was there, much less reach for me. I punched out with my spear, burying it deep in her chest, in her heart.

The crackle of energy from her hands faded, though they left charred fingerprints on the flesh of my wrist where she'd grabbed my spear hand after the hit. She took several shuddering breaths, let a final hateful hiss fly in my face, and dropped to the floor. Dead.

My spear stood stuck in her bleeding chest until it melted into rolling shadows and reformed in my hand once again, bloodless and clean. Handy trick. All the killing, none of the mess.

I would've taken a breath, thought about what I'd done, helped DD in some way, but there was no time. A deep rumble of a scream sounded above the mayhem in the hallway, and Wilbur came back through the door, a writhing clump of shadows in his bony, gnarled hand. He bounded toward the crack in the wall and tossed the wiggling form in with a strong heave and grunt.

Wilbur turned to me, his face bloodied by a deep gash on his forehead and already bruising all over from some serious physical or magical damage. Ny was nowhere in sight, and my confusion must have been clear because Wilbur curled his lip and threw a thumb to the crack behind him. "He tried to help you, the pitiful fool. Attempted to shadow walk back to the room when he felt your distress. Much easier to contain and expel his shadow form."

He bowed his head, as if pained by what he said next. "Nyarlathotep's weakness was always his care for you humans. Such a waste of power and position."

"You're half human yourself, dude," I countered, getting back into a low fighting stance, trying to prepare for whatever he'd throw at me.

"A trait I plan to remedy. But your weakness, Miranda, is you are all human. A condition you cannot help, and one which makes you so easy to tame."

"Better human than some uptight monster wishing it could play in the big leagues. Don't take your weird-ass daddy issues out on the rest of us, okay?"

He sneered, power wafting off him, but I was pushing back with my own, letting my thrum turn to a strong, steady beat to keep myself tuned up for a fight. "Nyarlathotep squanders your power because of his base sentimentality. I'll mold you into something more, something grand."

"You're not molding shit," I yelled, not liking how he talked about Ny but, more importantly, how he talked about me. As if I were a tool, something to be wielded and discarded without thought. Probably the way he thought of Macy, whose body still lay on the floor. A body he never even looked at when he came back into the room. I might have killed her, but Wilbur had led her to it every day of their miserable lives together.

"I am persuasive. My partner even more so. You will bend to us, or you will break. Either serves our purpose."

"Screw you, your partner, and your purpose. I'll die before I let you use me in any way."

"Oh, you'll die. All the others will die as well. Some sooner than others. Gareth Davis, Harley Warren, Merry Carter. I have no use for them. They will find death quickly. Mia Carter, on the other hand. Such an interesting and enterprising young woman. A woman who completed the Necronomicon and did not flinch at what it cost her. A woman I could use for a number of important ends."

I had no idea what he meant by Mia completing the book, or the cost of doing it, but it didn't matter then. All that mattered was this dude could not leave this room. My mind screamed at all he said, but I managed a strangled reply. "You will not touch any of them."

"You will be in no position to stop me." As he said this, he reached his arm deep into the crack and brought it back with a basketball-sized thing in his grasp.

The horror of the thing was too much for me to take in at first. It was a tinier but no less terrifying version of the thing I'd confronted during the tornado on Merry's twenty-seventh birthday. The thing that had made me swear off using the shadow world for years. It was an undulating mass of slippery tentacles, mouths, teeth, and eyes. So many, all over. So unreal and indescribably wrong, it made my flesh crawl to see it.

Wilbur stood there with it engulfing his hand, staring down at the thing without any sign he wanted to run screaming from the room. It took everything in me not to shadow walk my ass right out of the house, but I couldn't. I needed to finish this, especially if I was the last one left to stand against Wilbur.

"I still have plans for you, but much can be accomplished with a small portion of your person." Then flung the ball to the floor with enough force I physically felt the thud of its impact. For a second, it sat there unmoving, until it shuddered and pulsed, causing a wet, stretching sound to fill the strained silence as it grew to twice its original size in a blink. Then it moved, slithering my way impossibly fast. I stood frozen in place by fear and memory. Luckily for me, I wasn't the actual last man standing. Gareth came up from behind in time to empty what sounded like the entire clip of a gun into the mass of horror headed straight for me.

"Told you bullets have their uses," he muttered as we watched the bloody, oozing thing come to a standstill inches away from my feet.

# Twenty-Seven

WILBUR DIDN'T BLINK AT the massacre of tentacles and teeth and eyes and blood on the floor. Hadn't flinched at the gun fire. I did both but managed to pull myself together to stand tall by Gareth as he squared off against the man who'd killed his friends so long ago.

"Foolish to enter here," Wilbur crooned in a silky voice.

Gareth didn't reply. He pulled back and hit Wilbur with a blast of dark, shimmery magic—magic that looked a whole lot like Ny's eyes. Wilbur was surprised, all right. He dove away at the last second, but it caught a piece of his lower back. He gave a quick yelp but recovered himself, despite the smell of burning meat filling the space.

"You've come a long way, boy." Wilbur stood from his dive and sized up Gareth. "Before, you were nothing special. Another sheep to be culled for a greater purpose. Now, you have access to power you never imagined before. You might thank me for making you something better than your average human."

"You murdered people I loved in front of me. Nearly killed me." A dark look fell over his face, his voice so deep it was barely audible. "You'll wish you'd finished the job."

Another blast of power came from Gareth, but Wilbur was a smart opponent. He saw it coming and easily side-stepped. It fizzled at the end, and Gareth sagged slightly. He looked okay, but it was more than probable he was out of juice.

A dismissive laugh rang in the room. "Power you got from the ever-misguided Nyarlathotep. And power you waste foolishly. I was wrong. You're little better than you were."

"And you're a thing with so little power you can't take down a tired mage and a woman who started learning magic weeks ago," Gareth countered, hitting him right in the ego, right where a man like Wilbur would feel it most. I might've been offended if I wasn't internally cheering Gareth on, hoping he got in every real and figurative hit he could against this monster.

"I'll end you here and now, but not before you watch me take another person you love and drag them away, kicking and screaming." Before we could react, he reached once again into the crack in the wall and flung another monstrosity our way.

Gareth didn't reach for the gun this time around, apparently having emptied it into the first one. It squirmed at an alarming speed toward his thick boots and bit up his legs. He let out a horrendous howl of pain.

It all happened so quick, I had little time to think. I skewered it with my spear. When I pulled back, it wriggled on the end, still chomping and blinking and writhing to be free, to get at us. I didn't have time to think or plan. I felt the pull of my magic and tugged, hard, on whatever power I could find in the room. DD was recouping, but the tentacles of shadows from the crack in the wall came at my call. Surprised the hell out of Wilbur, who attempted to wrangle them back. He failed.

I hesitated, fear of the thing and the power it might give me, or the cost of the power it offered, slithering across my mind as it moved across the floor, the walls, and the ceiling to meet me. I had no time, no other options, so I gathered all the darkness to me. As I felt myself deepen and change in some odd way, power riding roughshod through my senses, Ny emerged from the crack and tackled Wilbur to the ground.

The shock of it managed to focus me back on task, kept me from falling into the unknown dark shadow. Instead, I sent the darkness out of my body, forcing it into the ball of horrid things trying to wiggle free from my spear. The dark shadow tentacles met real tentacles, but they were no match. The darkness dove deep, filled every nook and cranny of the nightmare

ball, and splintered it apart from the inside out like a
lock I could manipulate, undo without much thought.

"Your eyes," Gareth whispered, and I blinked at him.
I had no idea what he meant, but I shook it off and
looked back at Wilbur and Ny, who were wrestling on
the ground.

I tried to help, send those darker shadows out toward
Wilbur, but he broke free, kicking Ny so hard, he went
skidding across the room. I ran to him, but he was on
his feet, looking completely unharmed, when I skidded
to a stop in front of him. Maybe he'd have recovered
much more quickly and ended all of this if I hadn't
gotten in his way.

My move toward Ny gave Wilbur an out, and he
took it. He was halfway through the crack in the wall,
yelling his frustration as he ran away. He must have
known he was done if he stayed, because he sealed
the wall behind him, leaving a smooth, completely
unmarred surface in his wake.

"Dammit," I screamed, throwing my spear down in
my frustration. "Not fucking again. How the hell did I
let him get away? It's the same shit all over again!"

The house screamed along with me. Or groaned,
more like, beginning to shake on its foundations.

Ny, a little breathless but otherwise good, grabbed
onto me and Gareth, tugging us toward the door.

"We have to follow," Gareth said, wanting at Wilbur
again.

"Look!" Ny yelled, pointing at the walls, where the equations now ran down like molten lava. Sparks flew, and a small fire started on one patch of plaster. "The keys are pulling free because the person who anchored them no longer has access to this particular point on the plane. Wilbur is gone from us. For now. Soon, the house will be in flames. We must leave."

Fear and rage mingled in me at the thought of Wilbur's escape and all the mess we were still very much in because he probably wasn't gone for good, but I also heard Ny's warning. Saw the flames licking the old, dried, probably highly flammable walls. I didn't need to be told twice. I spared one last glance at the woman I'd killed, called DD and told it to hover close, and ran like a mad woman from a burning attic. I'd have waited, but I felt Gareth and Ny close behind, so there was no need. We were all running, then all out, staring at the house from across the street as flames licked up one grimy window on the second floor. It didn't take long to spread. We stood, half-dazed, and watched the house burn as neighbors gathered to stare and sirens wailed in the distance.

# TWENTY-EIGHT

NY DID HIS THING with the neighbors and the cops. Don't know if it was actual magic or him oozing sexy charm. Either way, we left without any questions after we watched the roof of the house cave in on itself and the firemen pulled back to do a more controlled burn. They were more concerned with bystanders and nearby structures than the creepy, old, deserted house itself.

Gareth and I jetted back to Harley's place, where we found Ny waiting, looking fresh and new in a clean version of his usual semi-goth leather-jacket, dark jeans, and shirt. He held a bag up as we approached, offering me my own fresh clothes. And thank the man, he hadn't tried to get me something pretty. It was a comfy T-shirt and well-worn leggings. Exactly what I wanted.

"Didn't know if I could get past your wards," Ny said, offering Gareth a form of an apology for not getting him fresh clothes too.

Gareth waved him off, intent to enter and get the scoop from Harley.

Merry and Mia bounded out of the condo door and crushed me in a sister hug I gave right back. Anger, frustration, hope, relief, and exhaustion all mixed together in my tears, and I had no words. They didn't need them. Seeing me, my griminess, and my emotions, they hurried me to Harley's office bathroom and gave me space to decompress.

I looked hard at myself in the mirror. My face was splattered with dirt and blood. A large bruise from a hit I didn't remember landing was spread across my forehead. A cut on my cheek wasn't bleeding anymore, but it looked heinous—angry, red, and swollen. My hair was a tangled dark halo around my head. The eyes though. It was hard to call them my eyes. They were distant, harsh, and maybe a bit cold. They were worn and tired. They'd seen more shit in an afternoon than some saw in a lifetime. I remembered Gareth's whispered awe about my eyes and made a note to ask him about it. Later. I said and thought the word "later" too damn much. Later would catch up, probably much sooner. But not then.

In the moment, I set the lid down on the toilet, put my head in my hands, and wept. For what I'd seen, what I'd done, and what I might have lost in doing it. For what was still ahead of us because Wilbur got away. What more days like today might turn me into over time.

AFTER CLEANING UP IN Harley's sink and getting into my comfy clothes, I strolled out of the bathroom, feeling a little more, if not fully, human.

I tossed my gross clothes in a heap on Harley's gleaming wood floor and said, "Burn these," to no one in particular.

Harley gave me a knowing look and a nod, likely understanding far more than my sisters what I'd went through in the past few hours. Merry, however, didn't let me slide.

"Pick those up right now, Miranda Love," she said. "Were you raised by wolves?"

I sure growled like a wolf at Merry's tone and her use of the first and middle. Very uncool on her part.

"Love?" Gareth and Ny both said at once, each putting a little too much emphasis on it.

I flipped them off without answer and, cutting Merry murder-eyes, bent to scoop my clothes off the floor. "Can you at least tell me where the trash is, Meredith Joy?"

Mia laughed out loud and muttered, "Before you two come to blows," as she took the bundle of ruined fabrics from my hold and marched upstairs, toward the kitchen and a trashcan.

I knew Merry didn't mean it. She'd been worried, strung tight for hours. Her snapping was understandable. I deflated, my anger seeping out, and shuffled to sit cross-legged on the plush rug in Harley's office.

Ny frowned at me and blinked away for a millisecond, coming back to my vision next to a pile of new camping chairs. I shook my head and said, "Unnecessary."

"I beg to differ," he replied, his voice and eyes both full of concern. For me. Because I'd broken down a little bit, then argued with my sister. Great.

I didn't argue. Rather, I let him pull me up, pop out a chair, and ease me back down in it. The folding camping chair things were great not only to cart around at festivals but also for lounging in a magical-training space after a horrible battle. Who knew?

Ny and Gareth, both gentlemanly in their separate ways, handed out chairs. Harley chose to stand, cross armed and hard faced, ready to talk business. I looked from her to Ny, wondering about how she felt with him in her space, how she'd let him through her wards to be here, to help all of us. "Thank you," I said when her eyes hit mine. The thanks was for a lot: letting Ny in and showing her trust of him, taking care of Merry and Mia, and her general badass help in all things.

"Of course," she said to me, echoing the same words she'd used weeks ago, the night before a different battle. A nod to her remembrance, her promise she'd keep helping through any and all days like this. My tears sprang up again at the memory and assurance, but I managed to tamp those down with a little effort.

Once all who would take a seat were seated—name-ly the Carter sisters and a now-lounging Ny—we re-hashed. Gareth told his version of events. He'd waited outside the house until he'd been too worried by the crashes and growls from inside, then broken down the front door, coming to my rescue with his handy handgun in the nick.

Ny explained what had happened to him. Wilbur had been able to get at him because he'd chosen to protect me. I protested, but he stopped his tale to wink and say, "It was no real choice, sweetling." When Wilbur had flung him into the wall, which he said was another transitory plane like and unlike the shadow world I knew, he'd had to materialize and fight off a few of those small horrors himself before he could get back to us.

After him, I went, telling my version of events. I spoke in a steady voice through most of it, but there was definitely some shakiness when I told them all how I'd killed Macy. I expected judgment, horror, or the like. Maybe didn't exactly expect it, but wouldn't have been surprised to see it. I found none. Harley, Gareth, and Ny looked on with an understanding that made my heart hurt for all of us. Merry and Mia looked at me with worry and love. I managed to once again strangle the sobs threatening to climb up my throat and finish telling my story.

Harley relayed the events in the apartment, which, with the exception of some pretty magical lights and sounds, had gone off without a hitch. Uneventful in the best possible way in my mind. However, after we were all filled in on the day's events, I was stuck on something.

"Wilbur said something about you completing the book."

Mia squirmed, and I knew instantly she'd done it. "How? Why? When? When were you even going to tell us? He said something about a cost. What did it cost? Oh my God, Mia! And Wilbur knows about it! He'll come after you. He wants it. He wants you."

I may have been panicking a bit, pulled into a frenzy by real and valid worry and the trauma of the day. Gareth stepped up, placing his warm, heavy hands on my shoulders, offering me a piece of the peace I felt when he was near.

Ny cut into my tirade with his smooth voice. "An issue we will deal with after some rest."

I closed my eyes, tried to reach for focus in the panic. The soft buzz of a familiar darkness helped. DD stroked my cheek as I managed to keep breathing, in and out, until I could think around the panic again.

When I opened my eyes again, Mia mumbled, "I'm sorry," pulling herself down in her chair, making her petite frame even smaller.

Harley glared at her and said, "We'll talk about this shit soon. For now, is there anything we need to do immediately?"

"No," Ny answered. "The house is gone. Macy and the familiar are dead. Wilbur has run to an inbetween space, likely back to his benefactor. The loss of the house, and the access keys there, will hinder his ability to freely travel between planes. We won't see him for some time."

"How long?" I asked.

Ny shook his head. "I'm sorry, sweetling, but I cannot say. All depends on his power, what he did in other areas of this plane, and the power and abilities of his benefactor."

"A benefactor who isn't his father," I replied, having forgotten the piece of info Wilbur spilled in the heat of the moment.

"So he implied, but we cannot be certain who backs him in the Dreamlands until we have more solid proof."

"He'll come back," I said, my voice sounding hollow even to my own ears.

"Yes," Gareth replied, "and we'll be waiting. Ready to take him on. Finish this once and for all." His fist was clenched on my shirt, and I reached up a hand to pat his, reassure him as he had reassured me moments before. For us, for him, and for his friends and all the people Wilbur hurt, we'd figure out a way to stop him permanently. We had no other choice.

WE HUNG AROUND HARLEY'S place for a little while, but not too long. I wanted to be home. Needed to feel my space around me, smell cookies and croissants and coffee, and get some grounding and comfort from my home. Gareth and Ny wanted to come, and I had no problem with them joining me. Mia offered to drive, so I figured she wanted to go as well. Maybe Merry and Harley needed some alone time together anyway after our day. I knew I needed something, though not to be alone necessarily. My littlest sister, a hunky, calming librarian, and a protective Outer God would do fine.

Mia and I didn't talk on the ride from Short North to Old North. It wasn't a long trip, but the silence stretched anyway. When she pulled into the one free spot in the tiny lot behind Warm Regards, she put the car in park but didn't turn off the engine. "Can I come in? Stay the night?" Her voice sounded small. I didn't like it.

"Sure, Mia. Always."

She chewed her lip, then looked at me with dark eyes—her usual dark brown, true, but also those newly minted bags lingered. Mia didn't look great, and I wanted to know why. She didn't make a grand confession. Instead, she asked, "You mad at me? You know, for keeping up with the book thing when I said I wouldn't?"

I heaved out a sigh. "Maybe. Doesn't mean I won't let you stay here whenever you want to stay. Or help you get through whatever you need to get through."

She shook her head, as if trying to drive out some bad thought or memory and whispered, "I should've listened."

Shit. That didn't sound good. I reached across the middle console, not caring about the weird slant of my body, and took her in my arms. We hugged each other awkwardly for long minutes. We both needed it. Finally, I whispered in her hair, "Want to talk about it?"

"Not yet. Not today. But soon. Promise."

Mia would. She'd own up to what she did, spill all the beans, and we'd deal with it. Now, we all needed rest and peace. Some may say we shouldn't put off until tomorrow what could be done today. They'd never had to fight evil cults, demigods, or creatures straight out of nightmare land, so those people could shove it. What we could put off for tomorrow might save our sanity today.

Eventually, we exited Mia's car. Ny and Gareth waited patiently, saying nothing, giving us whatever we needed. Whatever I needed. We all tramped up to my place. I made sandwiches from some baguettes I had around, and we ate in front of the TV in companionable silence. Together but not needing to speak. Finding comfort in taking up the same space.

When it was time for bed, Gareth, Ny, and I didn't talk about arrangements. I said I wanted to go to sleep, the two men looked at me with questions in their eyes, and I gave a chin lift toward my room in reply. Mia also didn't make a peep about it. She did give me a small smile and said she'd be sleeping on the couch–with her headphones over her ears.

I snorted. Tonight was not a night for those types of noisy good times, but I did want Ny and Gareth close. They followed me into my dark room, let me dive under the covers without turning on a light, then followed. Gareth snuggled, warm and calm on my right. Ny slipped into bed on my left, his zap of power a form of physical metaphysical reassurance. They both held me, without making demands. It was nice. More than nice, really. Something I wanted and needed. Maybe something I'd want more of later, but that was for another day, when I hadn't killed someone. When I could close my eyes and not see bloody horror. As I was squashed between the two men in my king bed, trying but failing to drift into dreams, I hoped the day would happen in the near future.

Please take a moment to rate *Shadow in the Witch House* on Amazon (https://www.amazon.com/dp/B0BRR24V G4). Every rating/review helps!

If you liked what you read and want more, consider preordering Book 3, Shadow in the Dreamlands, on Amazon (https://www.amazon.com/dp/B0BXFK95 6F) right now.

Also stay up-to-date with all things Sonya Lawson at sonyalawson.com.

# WANT MORE?

Interested in what Nyarlathotep was up to before he walked into Warm Regards? Join my newsletter and get a (very steamy) prequel story featuring the Prince of the Dreamlands. Visit BookFunnel (https://BookH ip.com/HNSGPTJ) to download the free story.

And don't forget to preorder Book 3, *Shadow in the Dreamlands*, on Amazon today! It will drop July 14th, 2023, so visit https://www.amazon.com/dp/B0BXFK95 6F now to make sure you get it as soon as it's released.

Want to read other books by Sonya Lawson? Check out more of her book pages below:

The Comus Duology

In Dreams of Dragons

# ACKNOWLEDGMENTS

The ladies at Novel Nurse Editing, Janna and Angie, deserve all the praise for their amazing editing skills. I'm a better writer every day because of them.

100 Covers once again knocked it out of the park with the cover design, and I'm so happy they're able to bring Randy to life for the eBook and paperback covers.

I dedicated this book to Lynn, who is an amazing friend in Columbus. I miss her all the time and hope to see her again soon.

All my writer friends help me grow in craft and business constantly, so thanks for all the time and care you put into helping me along.

Ario is a rock who lets me be me, and me do me, so I'm forever thankful for him.

I love "Dreams in the Witch House," even though a lot of Lovecraft fans don't like it. It's not one of his less popular stories, but something about it has always resonated with me. Maybe the fact it's about a grad student who slowly goes insane and references Salem witches, something I myself studied as a grad student. Whatever it is, I'm thankful for a weird, intense, and inspiring story.

# About Author

Sonya Lawson is a recovering academic currently writing steamy modern fantasy with maybe a few too many literary references. Her stories may differ, but they all have at least one common characteristic — sassy, intelligent women trying to do the best they can in whatever world they inhabit.

While she remains a rural Kentuckian at heart, she's spent a lot of time in the Midwest and currently lives in the Pacific Northwest. She fills her days with writing, editing, reading, walking through old forests, and watching sitcoms or horror films with her husband. Two rowdy cats terrorize her house regularly, but she loves it.

You can find more information about past books, current projects, and upcoming releases at www.son yalawson.com.

Don't forget to follow her on all her socials to stay connected. Find her on TikTok, Instagram, and Facebook using her username @sonyalawsonwrites.

Made in the USA
Columbia, SC
27 October 2024

45171535R00167